Daring Wings

Graham M. Dean

Alpha Editions

This edition published in 2021

ISBN : 9789354547355

Design and Setting By
Alpha Editions
www.alphaedis.com
Email - info@alphaedis.com

As per information held with us this book is in Public Domain. This book is a reproduction of an important historical work. Alpha Editions uses the best technology to reproduce historical work in the same manner it was first published to preserve its original nature. Any marks or number seen are left intentionally to preserve its true form.

Contents

CHAPTER ONE	- 1 -
CHAPTER TWO	- 12 -
CHAPTER THREE	- 22 -
CHAPTER FOUR	- 26 -
CHAPTER FIVE	- 32 -
CHAPTER SIX	- 39 -
CHAPTER SEVEN	- 45 -
CHAPTER EIGHT	- 52 -
CHAPTER NINE	- 62 -
CHAPTER TEN	- 70 -
CHAPTER ELEVEN	- 76 -
CHAPTER TWELVE	- 84 -
CHAPTER THIRTEEN	- 92 -
CHAPTER FOURTEEN	- 101 -
CHAPTER FIFTEEN	- 107 -

CHAPTER ONE

"Some of our biggest news stories will break above the clouds. The skyways are going to unfold great tales of romance, of daring, possibly of banditry, but whatever it may be, we must have the stories. Do you want the job of getting them?" George Carson, the sandy-haired managing editor of the Atkinson News, fired the question at the reporter standing at the other side of his desk.

"Do I want the job?" There was amazement in Tim Murphy's voice. "Give me a plane and I'll bring you some of the best yarns you ever printed." His clean-cut features were aglow with interest.

"All right Tim," said Carson. "This afternoon the News will announce the first flying reporter. I thought you'd like the job. That's why we sent you to an aviation school—so we can have the jump on the Times and the Journal. They can hire plenty of aviators but it will take them time to train a first class reporter to fly."

Tim grinned and his blue eyes snapped. Even though he was one of the star reporters on the staff he liked the managing editor's indirect compliment.

"We've got a plane all ready for you at the municipal airport," went on the managing editor. "It's one of those new Larks with a Wasp motor that will take her along at 150 miles an hour. She's all ready to go. The sky's your assignment—go the limit to get your stories."

Tim hurried back to his desk where the half completed story of a down-town fire was still in his typewriter. He picked up a pad of notes beside his machine and turned to the reporter at the next desk.

"Finish up this fire story for me, will you Ralph? Here's all the dope and the city editor wants it for the noon edition."

"What's the big idea?" Ralph Parsons wanted to know.

"Big idea is right," fairly exploded Tim. "I've got a new job—flying reporter. Carson has just bought a dandy new plane and I'm going to pilot it and write the stories."

"Good, Tim. I don't blame you for being excited. It's a great chance. I'll finish up the fire story for you. Will you give me a ride if I run out after I'm through this afternoon?"

"Sure, Ralph, a dozen if you want them," and with that Tim seized his hat and dashed through the door of the big news room, down the stairs and into the street where he found one of the flivvers used by the reporters.

Fifteen minutes later Tim tucked his elongated legs into the cockpit of the trimmest little plane he had ever laid eyes on. He ran the motor up and down the scale, then gave it the gun, darted over the surface of the field, flipped the tail up—and the flying reporter was in the air.

It was a glorious feeling to be in the air—to be free of the smoke and smell of the city and for an hour Tim circled over Atkinson. High, then low, he dived, banked, zoomed and looped—did everything to test the flying qualities of the little plane. At the end of the test flight he was more than pleased. It was perfectly rigged.

Tim, an orphan who had joined the News after school days, had worked up from cub reporter to the police run and then up to special assignment writer. He had been sent to an aviation school three months before and while there had written a series of Sunday features on learning how to fly. Tim hadn't dreamed of being given a flying assignment but he had mastered the intricacies of an airplane with the same wholesome enthusiasm which characterized everything he did. That was one of the reasons why he was a star reporter in spite of his comparative youth, for Tim had just turned twenty-one.

The Lark was still swooping over the field when one of the cars used by News reporters dashed through the main gate of the big airport. Tim cut the motor, made a three point landing, and climbed out of the cockpit.

Ralph Parsons hopped out of the car and ran toward the plane. He shoved an extra into Tim's hands.

"TRANSCONTINENTAL AIR MAIL ROBBED; $200,000 TAKEN." The headlines, in heavy, black type, fairly screamed the story at Tim. In brief clear sentences he read how the eastbound mail plane, which had left Atkinson at midnight, had been found a hundred miles east near Auburn, a village in the valley of the Cedar River. The plane was a mass of tangled wreckage, its pilot dead, the registered mail sacks looted.

"Carson says for you to hump yourself and get over there before dark," said Ralph. "He wants a lot of copy for the early editions tomorrow. The roads over that way are practically impassable and we can't get enough of the details over the telephone. The air mail people are sending out a ship but we don't know when they'll be back. It's bad country to fly over, Tim, so be careful."

Ralph's well meant warning was lost on Tim. Calling a mechanic, the lanky young flyer swung his ship around, opened up the powerful motor, and sped down the field and into the air. The flying reporter was off on his first assignment.

The air was smooth and cool. The late winter sun glinted through the lazy clouds in the west and flashed off the crimson wings of the little plane. Tim headed straight east. Far behind him the Great Smokies reared their heads in a dim outline while a hundred miles ahead of his whirling propeller the Cedar River carved its way.

Atkinson, with its bustling streets, its busy factories and 200,000 inhabitants, was soon left behind. For almost an hour Tim held to his course. When he sighted the silver ribbon that was the Cedar River, he swung south until he picked up the village of Auburn. It was little more than a cluster of houses on the right bank of the mighty river.

There was no regular landing field at the village but Tim found a pasture a mile back from the river that looked large enough for his purpose. He stalled down, taking his time. There was no use risking a crackup with his new ship. The pasture was cuppy and there was a slough on one side but Tim killed his speed quickly after he set the Lark down and pulled up less than twenty feet from a fence.

Tim had sighted the wreck of the air mail in a timber patch half way to the village. After landing his own craft it took him less than ten minutes to find what was left of the mail. There was little in the pile of wreckage to resemble the sturdy, silver craft which had left the Atkinson airport the night before. It was just a heap of tangled wires and struts, scraps of canvas and twisted rods. It looked like a crackup, with the mail looted after the smash, but to Tim's carefully trained news sense there was something more. He couldn't have defined his feelings in so many words but he played his hunch and examined the remains of the big plane. He had almost completed his examination when something on the motor caught his attention. He bent over it and when he straightened up there was a new gleam of interest in his eyes.

With the aid of a farm boy Tim managed to get a fence post under the motor and half rolled it over. A few minutes more of hard work and he succeeded in removing several parts from the engine.

By the time the flying reporter had completed his task the light was fading fast and, satisfied with his survey of the wrecked plane, Tim hurried toward the village.

Auburn was small but friendly and he soon found out what little the residents of the valley knew.

The east bound mail usually roared over the village about 1 o'clock in the morning, speeding through the night at better than one hundred miles an hour. But that morning the mail plane had failed to go over. That, in itself, was not unusual, for occasionally bad weather forced the cancellation of the trip. Tim, by careful inquiries, learned that one old man, living about two miles from the village, had heard the sound of a motor. His attention had been attracted by the high-pitched drone for the song of the mail was a heavy throbbing that once heard is seldom forgotten.

It had been mid-day before a farmer had found the wreckage of the mail, its pilot trapped in the cockpit, the registered mail sacks, with a big shipment of currency, looted.

Tim had enough material for his first story. Using the one long distance telephone wire in the village, he got in touch with the News office in Atkinson and dictated a detailed story. To spice it up, he added a hint about a mystery plane. It would make good reading.

The flying reporter had scarcely finished telephoning when the heavy throbbing of the motor of a plane echoed from the clouds. Hurrying out into the street from the telephone office, Tim could discern the riding lights of a mail plane as the pilot, hunting for a place to land, circled over the village.

Tim hired a car and sped toward the make-shift field where he had managed to land his own plane. When he reached the pasture he hastily piled some brush at one end of the field and set it afire. Then he raced for the other end and swung the car around so that its headlights outlined the far boundary of the pasture.

The roar of the mail plane's motor lessened as its pilot cut his throttle and brought his craft down to earth. The big ship bounced and swayed, threatening once or twice to nose over, but the mail flyer jammed his wheel brakes on hard and succeeded in stopping before he crashed into the fence.

Tim left the car and hurried to meet the newcomer.

"That you, Tim?" boomed a deep voice from the cockpit of the mail ship as the new arrival shut off his motor.

Tim smiled. The voice was familiar and Tiny Lewis, who weighed some 250 pounds, eased his bulk gently to the ground.

"Thanks a lot, Tim," he roared. "I was sure in a pickle. Figured on getting here before dark but made a forced landing about 50 miles back when two of the spark plugs fouled and I had to replace them."

Before starting for the village, Tim and Lewis put tarpaulins over the motors of their planes and staked them securely lest some freakish wind upset their craft.

When they reached the little hotel and had ordered their dinner, Tim told Lewis all he knew about the wreck of the air mail. When he had completed his story, Tiny whistled.

"Looks bad," he admitted, "and I guess there isn't much that I can do except make arrangements here for them to crate up what's left of the plane and ship it in to Atkinson. The post office inspectors will be here sometime tomorrow and they'll take charge of the investigation."

"I expected they'd be on hand," said Tim, "but I've got a little hunch all my own I'm going to see through to the finish. If it works out as I hope, it will be a real scoop for the News."

"Here's wishing you luck, Tim," said Tiny. "I'm going to roll in now. I flew in from the west today with the mail and then they sent me on out here. It's been a long day but I'll see you the first thing in the morning. Good night."

"Good night, Tiny," replied Tim.

After the mail flyer had lumbered up to his room, Tim went out to the hotel porch where he had laid the salvaged parts from the engine. He picked them up and lugged them up to his room. There, under the yellow light from a kerosene lamp, he strained over the broken bits. When he finally completed his minute examination, there was a grim smile on his lips.

After breakfast with Lewis the next morning, Tim phoned the News office, and putting a bug in the managing editor's ear that he had stumbled onto a real clue, got permission to free lance for the rest of the day.

Tim carefully wrapped up the engine parts and carried them to the field where he loaded them into his plane. Lewis was busy supervising operations for the crating and shipping of the remains of the mail plane and with a wave of his hand, Tim dodged over the trees that bordered the pasture and headed for Prairie City, two hundred miles away, where the state university was located.

Noon found Tim closeted with the head of the engineering school of the university, an international authority on electricity. Tim told his story in quick, clear sentences and in less than fifteen minutes the famous scientist had a graphic picture of what must have taken place in the midnight sky over the Cedar River valley.

For two hours the flying reporter and the scientist worked behind closed doors while messenger boys hurried to and from the telegraph offices, delivering telegrams that were eagerly grasped and hastily opened.

By late afternoon Tim was winging his way back to Atkinson, a smile of conquest lighting up his face. In his pocket was a paper with the secret of the destruction of the air mail plane, in his mind was a plan to catch the sky bandits.

When Tim reached Atkinson and entered the big editorial office of the News, he found it deserted for it was early evening and the staff on an afternoon newspaper completes its work before 6 o'clock. A scrub woman, busy at one end of the long room, paid no attention to the flying reporter as he sat down at his desk.

Tim sat before his battered typewriter until far into the night, recording his strange story. He told how the mail plane, speeding through the night over the valley of the Cedar River, had fallen earthward in a death spin, its motor silent, its pilot paralyzed in his seat while over the twisting, falling plane hovered its destroyer.

In glowing language he pictured the scene that must have taken place. A plane loitering in the night over the hills and valleys of the Cedar River in the path of the air mail. Then the red and green lights of the mail as it flashed out of the west, a quickening of the vulture's motor, a short dash through the night, a flash of invisible death, the mail plane careening down—a dead and fluttering thing.

And Tim wrote more, much more—of how he had found the motor of the mail plane a congealed mass, the pilot's body a husk of a man, burned by a powerful but invisible electric ray.

Still Tim went on. He told how the invisible ray recently invented and of which little was known, could be shot from a small gun. He described how he had consulted the famous scientist at the state university and how together they had found that one of the few invisible ray guns in existence had been stolen. This, concluded Tim, must be the weapon of the sky pirates.

From then on Tim conjectured as to how one of the men in the bandit plane must have taken to his parachute and followed the mail earthward, robbed the registered pouches of their fortune in currency, and escaped in a waiting car.

He had just completed his story and was reading it over for corrections when the lights all over the editorial room flashed on and the managing editor, who had dropped in on his way home from a theater, trotted up to his desk.

Carson was reputed to be capable of scenting a good story a mile away and he devoured Tim's copy, but not without evident astonishment and several open expressions of his admiration for the flying reporter's work.

"It's great stuff, Tim, great stuff," exclaimed the managing editor when he had finished reading the story. "I'm glad I dropped in tonight. I'll edit it now and schedule it for the early mail editions tomorrow. It will certainly set the town talking."

"I wish you wouldn't print that story tomorrow, Mr. Carson," said Tim.

The managing editor, who had started for his desk, spun on his heels.

"And why not?" he demanded. "Didn't you just tell me it was all right?"

"The story is all right, Mr. Carson," explained Tim? "but if you print it tomorrow the gang responsible for the robbery of the air mail will never be captured. If you'll hold the story for twenty-four hours there's a good chance that they can be apprehended."

"Not much," snorted the managing editor, "at least not as long as they have the death ray machine."

"You're wrong there," persisted Tim. "It's not only possible that they can be captured, but if you'll give me permission to use the News' plane I think I can turn the trick."

Carson was too surprised for words and before the managing editor could regain his poise Tim continued, driving his argument home. For over an hour they talked in low, strained voices, with Carson openly protesting at times as Tim explained his plan. Finally the managing editor gave his consent and Tim arose to go.

"Good luck, Tim," said Carson, "I'll see the air mail people the first thing in the morning and fix everything up for you."

Dead tired, Tim went to his room and turned in, but sleep would not come. Through the rest of the night his mind pictured the lurking bandit plane, the helpless mail flyer, the death ray fired from the gun, and then the bandit drifting earthward to feast on the spoils of the wreckage. Tim turned and tossed, enraged that men should stoop to such villainy, that an achievement of science should be turned to such low ends.

All next day Tim and a crew of mechanics at the municipal field worked desperately on the Lark in a secluded hangar. Carefully they sheathed the motor cowling and the fuselage with thin layers of lead and zinc, alternately spreading them on for they were as thin as paper. By nightfall the crimson plane was half gray with the cockpit and its vital parts protected by the thin sheathing of metal.

The Lark was ready for the test and the chances were that it would come that night. The two previous nights had been clear as crystal with a full moon riding the sky. The pilots of the mysterious vulture of the air would not be abroad on such nights for the risk of detection would be too great. Now, however, a thin cloud film at high altitude had spread over the heavens, making an ideal night for another raid on the air mail. And there was no doubt in Tim's mind but that they would raid again. They had not the slightest reason to believe that their secret had been discovered and certainly the valuables carried nightly by the mail plane would lure them into further attacks.

Well, Tim was ready for them, but the thought of actually doing battle in the air gave him many a nervous chill as he waited that evening for the time to go into action.

A figure hurried across the field and toward the hangar.

"Tim! Tim!" called an anxious voice.

"Who is it?"

"It's Ralph. Where are you?"

"Here at the southeast corner of the hangar. Look out you don't fall into the ditch."

"Say Tim, what are you up to to-night?" demanded Ralph as he panted up to the hangar. "There are all kinds of wild rumors floating around the office. Carson's sitting at his desk watching the clock and getting whiter every minute."

"I'm going to catch the gang that robbed the mail the other night," said Tim quietly. He hoped that his voice did not betray his emotion for inwardly he was seething with excitement. The waiting was what got on his nerves. He was tense, eager to be in the air and away.

"I had a sneaking idea that's what you were up to," said Ralph. "Count me in on the expedition," he continued. "I stopped at the police station and borrowed one of Chief Flaherty's riot guns." From beneath the topcoat which protected him from the raw night air, Ralph produced a sawed-off shot gun, capable of scattering a veritable hail of lead in whatever direction it was aimed.

Tim laughed heartily at his friend's determination but his next words were not easy to say. Ralph and Tim had worked on many a story together and their bond of friendship was close, but Tim could not afford to risk any life other than his own.

"I'm sorry, Ralph," he said, "but I can't take you along tonight. You're not used to flying, and, besides, this is a one man game."

"But Tim, something might happen to you," protested Ralph.

"Something might," conceded Tim, "and then what would you do a couple of thousand feet up in the air and traveling at 100 miles an hour? No, Ralph, not to-night."

The roar of the mail coming in from the west halted their conversation and Tim turned to direct the work of the mechanics while Ralph, realizing his helplessness, watched the final preparations.

Just as the mail trundled to a stop the lights on the field blinked out. There were shouts and calls for flashlights and a minute or two later the mechanics started their work of servicing the plane. In ten minutes it was ready to continue its eastward flight.

The pilot, slouched in his cockpit, waved for the mechanics to pull the blocks and gave his ship full throttle. Down the field he sped, then leaped into the air. His riding lights were disappearing in the east when the field beacons flashed on again.

Speeding into the night at one hundred miles an hour, Tim looked back and chuckled. In place of the regular mail plane, his own trim, fast little craft was rocketing eastward with dummy sacks of mail. It had been carefully camouflaged to look like the regular plane and when the lights went out, the larger ship had been pushed into a hangar and Tim's wheeled out in its place.

In less than another hour Tim would know just how good his theory and plans had been. He was willing to stake his life on them. The night air was exhilarating. Tim didn't want to die; in fact, he had no intention of doing so. As he raced through the scudding clouds, he carefully checked his plans. Ahead of him two long black machine guns peered over the edge of the cockpit.

For nearly an hour the racy little ship flew through the half clear night. When Tim sighted the curving light line that was the Cedar River, he eased the throttle. His greatest assignment was just ahead—if the air raiders were waiting!

Tim cut his speed to that of the regular mail plane. His riding lights glowed brightly. The young flyer tensed; eager for the test.

Whrrrrrr! A roaring black plane flashed from the clouds above, it powerful motor spitting flame. Tim's heart leaped. His mind was racing madly.

The black plane bore down on him. Tim ducked, and the vulture of the skies stormed past. Tim's own plane held its course. He had escaped from the invisible death. Instead of falling, a wisp of humanity in a lifeless plane, he was hard on the tail of the bandits' plane.

Tim pushed his little craft hard. The bandits, amazed that the first attempt had failed, were startled when the usually sluggish mail doubled its speed and took after them.

The gap between the two planes closed rapidly. Tim, crouched behind his guns and protected from the invisible rays by the lead and zinc which covered the cockpit, waited. Ahead loomed the black plane, its two astonished occupants glancing back at him.

Tim tripped his machine guns and a stream of tracer bullets, singing their song of death, streaked the blackness of night with threads of sparkling crimson as they coursed through the sky.

The black plane dodged this way and that, but always Tim was at their heels. He flew with the fury of a man possessed. Again and again it seemed as though the black plane must be destroyed by the leaden hail but each time its pilot managed to escape.

Tim zoomed quickly, the nose of his ship pointing into the belly of the bandit craft. Suddenly, with a grinding chatter, his guns jammed and his exultation became maddening disappointment. The chased became the chaser, and Tim was now on the defensive.

His plane had withstood one attack of the death ray but a second time the bandits might find a vulnerable spot. The pilot of the black ship quickly realized that Tim's guns had jammed and that his nervy pursuer was at his mercy. He lost no time in banking swiftly to make quick work of Tim.

The flying reporter, a desperate plan in his mind, cut his motor and drifted. It was his only chance and Tim staked the success of his midnight venture on a slender possibility. The bandit plane was storming down on him.

Again Tim ducked, again the breathless moment and again the thin covering of lead and zinc saved him from death.

The bandits, completely bewildered by the plane and pilot who defied destruction, slowed down. It was Tim's chance. Savagely he jammed the throttle on full. The Lark leaped and quivered, a roaring, pulsating king of the air. It was eating up the space separating the two planes. Tim's brain was in a whirl. Did he dare, would he succeed, what would happen if he failed? But the die was cast; he was almost on the black destroyer.

Hastily he loosened his safety belt, climbed to the edge of the cockpit and before the startled bandits could aim their death ray gun at him, leaped into space.

Then the planes crashed. As Tim floated downward, his parachute billowing out above, he heard the scream of breaking wires, the crash of struts, the last wild, defiant roar of speeding motors as his own plane ate its way into the other. To his left Tim could see two other parachutes drifting earthward. The bandits had not been caught in the crash!

CHAPTER TWO

While the parachutes floated down through the night, Tim realized that things were not turning out the way he had expected. He hoped the posse which was supposed to be in readiness at Auburn had seen the battle in the sky and was ready to do its part now.

Tim spilled some of the air from his parachute to speed his descent. He must reach the ground ahead of the bandits. If the posse wasn't on the job, he might be able to handle the situation alone. Below him a heavy patch of timber loomed in the night. He jerked hard on the chute cords and, kicking desperately with his legs, swung away from the trees and dropped into a small clearing. Over to his right he could see the other two parachutes settling to earth.

The flying reporter unsnapped his parachute harness, made sure that his gun was ready, and then sprinted toward the place where he had last seen the parachutes.

There was a rushing, moaning sound that stopped Tim in his tracks. For the moment he had forgotten the two planes. Locked together, they had swung in great circles in the sky and the flyers, who had leaped in the chutes, had beaten them to the ground. Now, in a last tragic circle, the planes were hovering over the trees. For a moment they hung in the sky. Then, with a final flirt of their tails, stuck their noses down and the next moment struck the ground with terrific impact. There was a flash of fire and the roar of bursting fuel tanks. In a moment both planes were masses of flame.

Tim groaned at the thought of his beloved Lark coming to such an end and he hurried on with renewed determination. A hundred yards on the other side of the burning planes he came to an open field. Two irregular masses of white were laying near the center while on the far side Tim could distinguish the forms of two men, running toward a nearby road.

He heard the sputter of a powerful engine, headlights flashed on and before he was a third of the way across the field a car, with the two aerial bandits in it, was speeding down the valley away from the village of Auburn.

When the posse arrived five minutes later they found Tim waiting for them at the side of the road. Briefly he explained what had happened and then went to Auburn where he telephoned his story to the News office.

It was the next afternoon when Tim reached Atkinson and he half way expected a bawling out from Carson for the loss of his new plane. Instead, he found the managing editor jubilant.

"Best story we've had in months, Tim," congratulated Carson. "And the Transcontinental is going to replace our plane so you can go cloud-hopping again."

"I'm glad you liked the story," replied Tim, "And it's great of the Transcontinental people to buy a new plane, but I felt I sort of fell down on the story. I should have caught those fellows."

"Nonsense," exploded the managing editor. "It wasn't your fault the posse wasn't on the job. You did everything you could."

"Yes, I know," said Tim, "but it makes a fellow's blood boil to think of flyers who will stoop as low as that pair. Besides, they're apt to try the stunt again. Not with the death ray but with something else. The airways aren't patrolled like the highways and some mighty valuable cargoes are carried by plane these days."

"Kind of riles up your Irish pride at the thought of them getting away, doesn't it?" asked Carson.

"Guess it does," admitted Tim, "but you don't want to be too sure they've gotten away. Next time it will be a different story."

"I hope there isn't a next time," said the managing editor, and he picked up the handful of copy he had been reading when Tim came in.

News is news but for a day and then it fades from the front pages to become only a matter for memory, and so it was with Tim's adventure with the sky bandits.

For a few hours he received the praise of his fellow reporters. Then his deed was forgotten in the hurry and bustle that is part of a great daily newspaper. Tim would not have wished it otherwise. He had no desire to be a hero, even in the News office, and considered the entire incident as nothing more than a part of his duty, for reporting takes its followers into many a situation which calls for quick thinking and steady nerves.

In less than two weeks the new plane which the Transcontinental Air Mail company had agreed to buy to replace the one wrecked by Tim in the Cedar River valley arrived and was uncrated at the municipal field. The mechanics were busy several days assembling the plane and another day was required for the ground tests.

Then Tim was ready to soar into the clouds again. The test flight was successful and the flying reporter was highly elated with the new Lark. He was ready to follow new trails through the sky in his quest for the news of the day.

One morning a copy boy stopped at his desk.

"Say Tim, Mr. Carson wants to see you."

Tim's slender fingers stopped their tattoo on the keys of his typewriter. Anchoring his notes securely under a piece of lead he used for a paper weight, he left his desk and walked down the aisle in the center of the big news room. At one end, on a slightly elevated platform, were the desks of the managing editor and the city editor, so located that the executives in charge of the paper could see at a glance just what reporters were in the room. Directly in front of the platform was a large, horseshoe shaped desk where half a dozen copyreaders were busy editing stories which were to go into the editions that day. At the center of the horseshoe sat the head copyreader, a gray-haired veteran by the name of Dan Watkins, who could spin many a yarn of the early days.

The copyreaders, engrossed with their work, did not look up as Tim passed by.

"Sit down, Tim," said the managing editor, and he waved the flying reporter to a chair beside his desk. For a minute Carson was busy with the makeup editor, completing the final layout for the first page of the mail edition for that day. The layout finished, he turned to Tim.

"I'm well satisfied," he commenced, "with the way you're handling our plane. There's just one thing, though, Tim. Sometime you may not be able to take the controls and then we'll be up against it."

"But you could get any one of half a dozen reliable pilots at the municipal field to fly for you in an emergency," suggested Tim.

"I know it," replied Carson, "but I want more than pilots. I want flying reporters. When I first gave you the assignment of handling our new plane, I felt sure that many of the big stories of the future will be in the air. Now I'm more convinced than ever. What I want is another flying reporter; someone that can take your place if need be. I want you to pick your man from the staff and devote the next few weeks to teaching him how to fly. I've made arrangements with the manager of the municipal field to give you whatever assistance you need."

"That's fine, Mr. Carson," said Tim enthusiastically. "Does this mean you want me to take three or four weeks and give all my time to teaching someone on the staff to fly?"

"Right, Tim," said the managing editor. "Have you any suggestions? Pick your man carefully," he added, "for we have a heavy investment in that plane."

"I believe Ralph Parsons could be trained to fly," suggested Tim.

"But isn't Ralph a little too slow for this game in the air?"

"Ralph may be a little slow in learning," admitted Tim, "but he's steady and that counts a lot in flying. On top of that, Ralph is a brilliant and clever writer. I'm sure he would fit into your scheme of things nicely."

"All right, Tim," agreed Carson, "if you think Ralph can handle the job we'll give him a try. When he comes into the office tell him I want to see him."

Half an hour later Ralph breezed in from his round of the hotels. Without betraying anything unusual in his voice, Tim accosted his chum.

"Ralph, Mr. Carson wants to see you right away. It's important."

Ralph frowned. "Wonder what's up now," he said, as he started for the managing editor's desk.

Tim smiled for he knew how his chum would feel when he returned from the interview with Carson.

Five minutes later Ralph fairly ran down the room to Tim's desk. He was bubbling with excitement.

"Why didn't you tell me what he wanted," he exploded. "Gosh, Tim, I'm so tickled I hardly know what to do."

"I'm mighty glad, too," said Tim. "It's a great opportunity and I know you'll make good. We're to take three or four weeks and go in for an intensive course."

When they reached the municipal field the next morning, Tim took Ralph to the office where he introduced him to Carl Hunter, the genial manager of the field.

"So you're going to be the new flying reporter," smiled Hunter as he greeted Ralph. "That's great. Tim phoned me yesterday and I've got a ship all ready and waiting on the line for you chaps."

Ralph was a little disappointed when he saw the craft in which he was to take his first lesson. It was an antiquated machine whose exact number of years were unknown. Suffice to say that it was classed as a "Jenny," a type of biplane used by the army in training it's flyers in the days of the World War.

The Jenny's wings drooped a little dejectedly and her fuselage was liberally patched and doped but the motor, which was turning over slowly, sounded sweet.

"Everything O.K.?" asked Hunter as Tim completed his examination of the plane.

"Looks like it," said the flying reporter, as he turned to his chum to explain the intricacies of a seat pack parachute. With the heavy package banging around his knees, Ralph climbed into the rear cockpit. The instruments there looked sensible enough to him. A gas gauge to indicate the amount of fuel, an altimeter to show the height, an oil gauge to show that the motor was getting the proper amount of lubrication and a tachometer which indicated the number of revolutions of the motor per minute.

Tim was getting Ralph acclimated to the cockpit and he intentionally kept the motor idling while he explained the functions of the controls; how the rudder at the back of the fuselage controlled the right and left direction of the plane while the ailerons on the wings were used to direct it's up and down movements. The explanation seemed simple enough to Ralph and when he placed his feet on the rudder bar it recalled days not so long gone when he had guided a speeding sled down long hills. This might not be so bad, after all, but he admitted a few qualms when Tim climbed into the forward cockpit, strapped himself in, revved up the motor, waggled the wings, and sent the plane throbbing into the air.

Ralph needed some time to get used to the sensation of roaring along through the clouds at eighty miles an hour and for the first fifteen or twenty minutes Tim made no effort to give his chum any further instructions. Instead, they conversed freely through the headphones and Tim took pains to keep Ralph's attention diverted from the plane and its maneuvering. When he felt that his chum had become more air-minded he started the actual instruction.

Ralph was slow to learn the rudiments of handling the plane, but he was steady and after another half hour in the air, Tim took his hands off the controls and signalled for Ralph to take the stick. Everything went well for several minutes until they struck an air pocket and the ship dropped fifty feet. Ralph, surprised at the sinking sensation, overcontrolled and threw the Jenny into a side-slip.

Tim righted the plane and continued the instruction for another ten minutes. Then he started down, calling Ralph's attention to every shift in the position of the controls and explaining his reason.

When they skimmed to a stop in front of the office at the field they were stiff and numb from cold for the late winter winds had bitten through their heavy clothing.

Hunter was on hand to greet them.

"How goes it?" he asked.

"Fine, Carl, fine," said Tim. "Ralph will make a cracking good flyer when he gets over being scared. We'll be out again this afternoon."

Three weeks slipped away and to Ralph and Tim the time was like three days. Then Ralph was ready for his solo flight. He had satisfied both Tim and Hunter that he could handle a plane and that morning, late in March, he was to soar aloft alone.

Ralph, silent and serious of face, took his place in the Jenny. He heard Tim yell a few reassuring words at him. Then he was off.

Ralph got the Jenny off the ground like a veteran and started climbing for altitude. At 2,000 feet he levelled off and swung the Jenny over the field in great circles, his motor barking in the crisp morning air. For fifteen minutes Tim and Hunter strained their necks as they watched Ralph put the Jenny through her paces.

"He's all right," said Hunter, "you've done a nice piece of work, Tim, in teaching him how to fly. I was afraid he wouldn't be fast enough in an emergency." When the manager of the Atkinson field said a flyer was all right, he was that and more, for Hunter was known as a cautious man.

Tim and Hunter turned to glance at another ship that was being warmed up on the line. A shout from a mechanic brought their attention back to Ralph, and their faces went white at the sight of what was happening in the sky. Far above them the Jenny was twisting and falling. For a moment they were speechless.

"His right wing's crumpled," yelled Hunter. "He's going to crash."

Tim's throat tightened. He couldn't even speak when he realized what Ralph was up against. It was enough to turn a veteran pilot gray headed, much less a beginner making his first solo.

If Ralph could keep the Jenny out of a tail spin he had a chance, just a chance. Down, down, down, fluttered the crippled plane, so slowly and yet so swiftly. Nearer and nearer the field Ralph swung his battered ship, nursing it every foot of the way. At 500 feet it fell away in a steep glide—so steep that the two near the hangar held their breath.

The plane gained speed, the sideslip was steeper. In another second it would strike the ground, roll over, and crush its pilot. Tim turned away; he couldn't stand it.

Only Hunter saw Ralph stake his life in a desperate chance and saw him win. Just before the plane crashed he threw his controls over, bringing his left wing up and levelling off. The lower right wing held for the needed fraction of a second, just the time required to pull out of the sideslip, and Ralph set his crippled plane down hard.

Instead of a bad crash, it was only a noseover and by the time Tim and Hunter reached the Jenny, Ralph was scrambling out of the cockpit.

"Hurt, Ralph?" cried Tim.

"Not hurt, just scared," he grinned. "Guess I kind of smashed up the old bus, Carl," he went on, his words tense and close clipped. "I'm mighty sorry."

"That's all right, Ralph," said Hunter. "She was about at the end of her string and I guess I shouldn't have let you take her up for your solo. I'm glad it wasn't any worse."

"How did you feel coming down?" queried Tim, as they started back to the office after a careful survey of the wrecked Jenny.

"Pretty nervous," admitted Ralph, "but it's great stuff. I'd have been all right if I hadn't hit a bump when I went into a sharp bank and the old ship just couldn't stand the gaff. It was some trip down, though. I thought I had a ticket straight through for China."

"That landing with the broken wing was a great piece of flying," cut in Hunter in his quiet voice. Ralph was thrilled, for words of praise from the manager of the field meant much.

"Better come out this afternoon," said Hunter when they reached the office, "and we'll have another try at it."

Tim caught the significance of the words and he wondered if Ralph sensed their meaning. After a crash the first thing for a flyer to do is to get into the air again. If he lets the effects of the crackup work on his nerves he may never be able to handle a plane again. Tim realized that his chum had been through a severe flying ordeal but he was elated that Ralph had come through in such fine shape. The next thing was to get him back into the air as soon as possible and in the meantime to keep his mind occupied with thoughts other than those of the crackup.

They were speeding into town in one of the cars owned by the News when Ralph let out a yell and Tim swerved just in time to avoid a hog which was having a hard time making up its mind in which way to go.

"One thing," laughed Ralph when the pork menace was safely behind, "we don't have to dodge such things up there."

Tim purposely took Ralph to the busiest cafeteria in town where the rush to get food kept them busy for half an hour. The heavy tide of noonday traffic caught them in its swirl when they started back to the field and by the time they reached the airport, they had said scarcely a dozen words about the incident of the morning.

Hunter, wise in the ways of the air and the men who ride through its trackless lanes, had another plane warmed up on the line when they put in their appearance.

It was the work of only a few minutes for Ralph to don his heavy flying clothes. Tim thought his chum looked a little white around his lips. He wondered what thoughts were racing through Ralph's mind. If his chum only knew it, the big test was before him.

Tim wanted Ralph to make good, wanted him to pass the next ordeal for he knew how much he had counted on becoming a companion of the flying reporter. They had worked up from cub reporter, taken all the hard knocks of the newspaper game with a smile. Now their big opportunity was at hand if Ralph could come through the gruelling test of the afternoon. Tim knew he must go on flying even if Ralph failed, but the zest of it would be gone.

Ralph took his place in the cockpit of the ship Hunter designated. It was similar to the old Jenny in design but a much sturdier type. Tim watched Ralph closely as he checked over the instruments. If Ralph was upset or unnerved at the thought of taking the air so soon after his first crackup, he gave no sign other than a certain firmness to the lines around his mouth.

With a roar, Ralph went scudding down the field, bouncing from side to side. Tim felt chills of apprehension running up and down his back as Ralph jounced along. There was little in his handling of the plane to resemble the fine takeoff of the morning. But just before Ralph crashed into the fence at the other side of the airport, he pulled the stick back hard.

The little ship shot skyward in a breathtaking climb; almost straight up it seemed to the anxious watchers on the field. For a second it hung at the peak of its climb. Would it fall off into a spin or would the sturdy motor pull on through? For an eternity the plane was hanging almost vertically against the sky—then the nose came down, the tail went up, and Ralph started circling the field.

Again Ralph put his plane through its paces and as far as Tim and Hunter could see, his handling of the craft showed no sign of uncertainty. At the end of half an hour he had completed every maneuver and even more than is required of a pilot on his solo flight but instead of coming down, Ralph continued to circle the field.

For ten or fifteen minutes Tim thought little of his chum's actions but before the hour was up he was genuinely worried. What could be keeping Ralph up? he asked himself.

Hunter dodged out of the office to scan the sky.

"What's Ralph doing up there so long?" he asked Tim in surprise.

"I don't know, Carl," replied the flying reporter, lines of worry creasing his brow. "I'm going to warm up the Lark and hop up and see if anything is wrong."

In less than ten minutes, Tim, in the Lark, was pulling up beside Ralph's plane. Tim was astonished at the sight which greeted his eyes. Apparently the training plane was a ghost ship, flying without human hands at its controls. Ralph was nowhere to be seen! But the movements of the ailerons and the rudder indicated that someone was in the cockpit and Tim wondered what kind of a joke Ralph was trying to play on him.

The two planes circled lazily over the airport and when several minutes elapsed and Ralph still remained hidden in the cockpit, Tim felt new alarm. He let the Lark drop behind the training plane, then gave it the gun and climbed above Ralph's ship so he could look down into the cockpit.

He could see Ralph, doubled up on the floor at one side of the cockpit, controlling the plane as best he could with his hands. Ralph evidently heard the deeper roar of the motor of Tim's plane for he looked up and managed to wave one hand. His face was twisted with pain.

The flying reporter waved back at his chum, then threw the Lark into a sideslip and plunged madly for the ground.

Hunter heard the thunder of the Lark as Tim sent it earthward in a power dive and was waiting for the flying reporter when he checked his plane on the concrete apron in front of the office.

"Something's happened to Ralph," yelled Tim. "He's slumped down in one corner of the cockpit. Evidently he can't use his legs for he's handling the controls with his hands. We've got to get him down some way or he'll crash sure."

Hunter glanced at his watch. "He's been up nearly an hour and a half and I didn't put much gas in that ship," he muttered half to himself and half to Tim.

Tim slipped into the forward cockpit and yelled for Hunter to take the controls. A mechanic helped them whip the Lark around and get it headed down the field.

Hunter opened the throttle wide. The Lark had its tail off the ground in a hundred feet and in less than five hundred feet was pointing its nose into the sky.

While they fought for altitude, Tim slipped the harness of his parachute from his shoulders. He couldn't afford to be hampered by anything as cumbersome as a parachute if his plan to save Ralph from crashing was to succeed.

Tim and Hunter quickly overtook Ralph's plane and that young man, despite the seriousness of his predicament, managed to grin at them as they jockeyed for a position directly over him.

While Hunter was coordinating the speed of the Lark with that of the training plane, Tim slipped out of his seat and down onto the wing. From the lower wing it was the work of a minute to wrap his legs around the landing gear and slide down onto the axle below the plane. If Hunter could bring the Lark down close enough to Ralph's ship, Tim planned to drop onto the upper wing of the training plane.

The Lark was hovering over Ralph's ship when the motor of the lower plane coughed once or twice and died. Not more than fifteen feet separated Tim from Ralph but it might just as well have been a mile. The training plane, its motor dead, was rapidly falling away from the Lark in spite of Hunter's best efforts!

CHAPTER THREE

Tim yelled until it seemed his lungs would burst but the roar of the Lark's own powerful motor drowned out his cries. Finally Ralph, who had been working desperately in the cockpit of his own plane, looked up at his chum. Death was staring him in the face, but there was no hint of fear in the eyes that gazed at Tim.

The flying reporter signalled Ralph to reach for the lever which opened the emergency gas tank. If there was fuel in the reserve tank, the motor might catch again and they would have another chance.

The lever which controlled the valve of the emergency tank was on the other side of the cockpit and Tim, hanging on his precarious perch, watched his chum strain to reach it. Ralph lunged toward the lever and his outstretched hands knocked it open. The fuel flooded down into the carburetor and hissed into the red hot cylinders. With a quiver the engine of the training plane came to life.

Tim couldn't restrain a shout as he saw Ralph gain control of the plane again.

Hunter lost no time in bringing the ships together and the Lark crept down and over the upper wing of Ralph's plane.

Tim steeled himself for the attempt. He had never tried to change from one plane to another but he had watched the stunt a dozen times. The feat looked easy then, but actually to attempt it with a friend's life in the balance was an entirely different thing.

Just ahead Tim could see the flashing arc of the propeller of Ralph's plane. If Hunter misjudged the distance, if they struck a bump, if—if any one of half a dozen things happened he might be thrown into the deadly whirl. But Hunter was a master pilot and——

Before Tim's madly racing mind could conjure up other thoughts they were over Ralph's plane. Six feet, five feet, four feet separated the under carriage of the Lark from the upper wing of the training ship. Tim released his hold on the axle.

The next moment the air was forced from his lungs as he sprawled against the surface of the wing. His desperately reaching fingers hooked themselves over the wires along the upper edge of the wing and he was safe.

Tim was stiff from the cold and bruised by his fall but he swiftly made his way in from the tip of the wing and crawled down into the forward cockpit. His action was not a moment too soon for the supply of fuel in the reserve tank was exhausted. He grabbed the dual controls in the forward cockpit and within thirty seconds had set the plane down on the field. Hunter, who had beaten him down, ran toward him and together they clambered into the rear cockpit.

Ralph's face was drawn with lines of pain.

"I guess I've made a supreme mess of things," he gritted, before they could ask him what had happened.

A doctor who had been summoned by one of the mechanics when Tim and Hunter went aloft, shoved Hunter aside and slipped into the cockpit beside Ralph, whose legs, useless, were doubled under him.

"Here you chaps," called the doctor, "help me lift this boy out of here." Together they hoisted Ralph out of the cockpit and carried him into the office where they laid him on a cot in Hunter's room.

The doctor's examination required only a few minutes and he was smiling when he turned to the others in the room.

"Nothing serious," he reassured them. "When he had that crackup this morning he bruised his legs pretty badly and also strained his back. The reaction took place this afternoon and resulted in a temporary paralysis of the legs. Keep him good and warm for an hour or two and he'll be O. K. His legs may be a little sore and stiff for a day or two but that's all."

The doctor picked up his things and departed. When he had gone, Ralph looked up at Tim, his eyes clouded with grief.

"I'm sorry I'm such a flop, Tim," he said. "I tried hard to make good because you told Carson I could do it."

"Make good?" exclaimed Tim. "Why Ralph, you're a flyer if ever there was one. It takes nerves and brains to do what you did this afternoon to keep a ship aloft with your legs paralyzed and your gas supply dwindling down to nothing. Believe me, that was flying."

The cold winds of winter had been replaced by the warmer breezes of early spring and clouds that had been heavy with snow unleashed their burden of rain. It was poor weather for flying and Tim, after checking over his plane, was preparing to leave the airport.

The deep humming of a powerful motor attracted his attention and he turned toward the sound. Out of the low gray clouds in the west a black monoplane flashed into view. It was coming fast and low. The craft shot over the field and as it flashed by, Tim noted that it was a dull black. The fact that there were no numbers indicating its department of commerce rating troubled him. Then the pilot of the unknown plane banked sharply, and with motor on full, sped back over the field.

An arm flashed over the edge of the fuselage and a white object floated down. Tim splashed across the muddy field and retrieved the letter from the puddle in which it had fallen. By that time the black plane had disappeared with only a faint drumming of its motor to tell of its passing.

The flying reporter held the letter gingerly. When he turned it over he was astounded to find that it was addressed to him. On the envelope, in a rough scrawl, were the words, "For Tim Murphy."

Tim tore open the envelope and extracted the single sheet of plain paper. The words were few but they burned their way into his mind.

"Murphy," he read, "you've spoiled my game once. Don't do it again." It was signed, "The Sky Hawk."

A queer feeling, certainly not that of fear, yet hardly that of elation, held Tim for a moment. So he had crossed the path of the Sky Hawk, the famous bandit who had been terrorizing the airways of the east. Tim smiled a little grimly. So far he had always been able to take care of himself and he had won his first tilt with the sky robber.

Stories about the Sky Hawk had been front page news some months before when he had staged a number of daring aerial holdups on eastern airways, but recently he had disappeared, which accounted for the failure to first connect him with the robbery of the Transcontinental Air Mail. There were many tales about the Sky Hawk. Some were that he was a super-flyer, a famous World war ace who had gone wrong; others had him leading a desperate band of aerial gunmen. One thing Tim knew; if the Sky Hawk had been piloting the plane which had attacked the mail, he had a number of accomplices.

The flying reporter walked over to the manager's office and laid the letter on Hunter's desk.

"I was afraid of something like that," said the airport chief when he finished reading the note. "The possibility of the Sky Hawk had occurred to me before but I thought I'd get laughed off the field if I mentioned it. You'll take good care of yourself, won't you, Tim?"

"Sure, Carl, and while I'm here I want to find out what you know about this flying circus that blew in a couple of weeks ago. Why didn't they stop at your field?"

"They landed here first but when they found we charged a percentage on all passengers carried, they pulled out and rented a pasture on the other side of town."

"Guess I'll drift over that way," said Tim. "There may be a story."

The flying reporter took the office car he had used to come down to the field and fifteen minutes later had skirted the edge of the city and reached a level tract of land where several canvas hangars had been erected. A sign over the gate announced that the "Ace Company" was ready for business. Tim turned his car from the main road and into the field. There was no one on duty at the gate and he started for one of the hangars where he could hear men at work.

He was about to push aside the canvas flap when a burly mechanic fairly jumped out of the tent.

"What you doing here?" he bawled.

"Just looking around," replied Tim. "I'm Murphy of the News?"

"Oh, so you're Murphy of the News?" mimicked the mechanic. "Well, we don't want any flying snoopers sticking their noses in here. Now get out and stay out!"

Tim appraised the mechanic. He was six feet or better and weighed a good two hundred pounds. To try to argue with him would be foolhardy and Tim turned and started for his car.

Halfway to the car he paused for a moment, a peculiar mark on the soft turf of the field attracting his attention. It was the mark of a tailskid and from its clean-cut appearance, must have been made within the last hour!

CHAPTER FOUR

On the way back to the office, Tim mulled over the events of the last few weeks. First the attack on the transcontinental air mail, then the warning note from the Sky Hawk, his gruff reception at the Ace air circus field and finally his discovery of the tailskid track on a day that was rotten for flying. Only a flyer with an urgent mission would think of flying with the weather conditions what they were and yet someone had evidently landed at the Ace field within the last few minutes.

Tim felt that the gods who hold the threads of fate were weaving a new pattern and that he was being drawn deeper and deeper into it. The flying reporter was seldom blue, but something in the air, the very grayish color of the day depressed him and he was moody when he reached the office.

"What's the matter, Tim?" asked Dan Watkins, the venerable head of the copy desk. "You look like you'd lost your last friend. Suppose you're mad because all this rainy weather is keeping you tied down and you have to associate with us earthworms." Dan chuckled at his own sally.

"I don't know what's the matter, Dan," admitted Tim. "I feel all restless and stirred up inside—unsettled."

The head copy reader looked intently at the flying reporter and what he saw in the usually clear blue eyes brought forth his next words.

"Get your hat, Tim," he invited, "and come out and have lunch with me. It will do you good to get out of this stuffy atmosphere."

Tim welcomed the invitation and Dan guided him down a side street to a cheery little restaurant. There was little conversation until they had given their orders for lunch.

On their way to the restaurant Watkins had carefully appraised Tim, recalled everything he could remember about the boy, and had reached a decision. He started the conversation over the white-topped table.

"I know what's troubling you, Tim," he began. "You're afraid you'll get in a rut. Right?"

Tim nodded, his eyes on fingers which were fumbling nervously with the silverware.

"I guess that's about right," he admitted, his voice low. "I don't want to be a flying reporter all my life and I'm afraid I haven't the background to get ahead. But there's something more than that." And Tim told the copy reader about the note from the Sky Hawk.

"Don't let that worry you, Tim," advised the veteran newspaper man. "It may be only a joke; it may not, but whatever it is, I have confidence you'll be able to take care of yourself. Right now there is something we want to thresh out. A minute ago you said you didn't think you had the background to get ahead. What do you mean by that?"

"Well, I've only had a high school education and it takes more than that to get ahead in the modern newspaper world. I've got a fine job now, piloting the new plane, but in a few years I won't be fast enough for that. Then what? Oh, maybe the weather has made me blue, but I've gotten into an awful muddle."

"I think you have," agreed the veteran of the copy desk, "and it looks like it's high time for your uncle Dan to straighten things out for you."

"I've seen lots of young chaps go through this same trouble," he went on. "Some of them snapped out of it while others went under. But listen to me, Tim," and there was rare charm and power in the words, "You must never let this thing get your goat. You're made of too fine material."

Tim started to reply but Dan waved his words aside.

"You have the opportunity of a lifetime," he continued. "Here you are—young, capable, and with aviation in its swaddling clothes. Within ten years it will be a giant among giants and the newspaper man who knows aviation from the ground up will be in an enviable position—a position to command real power and respect."

There was new interest in Tim's eyes and he drank in Dan Watkins' words.

"You're luckier than you know," added the head copy reader, "for you have behind you a great newspaper organization. Someday, and someday soon, the News will need an aviation editor. Someone who knows the air from A to Z, someone with nerves and brains and foresight, and there isn't a reason in the world why you shouldn't fill that editorial chair when the time comes. Don't get moody, don't get discouraged. I know the weather gets a fellow's nerves once in a while but you must learn to pull yourself over those rough spots."

"I think you're right about the future for an aviation editor," agreed Tim, "and that's one of the things that has put me in the dumps lately. The field is so big and I know so little about it. When the time comes to select an editor I'm afraid Carson will pass me by and pick a man with more education."

"You can remedy that, Tim," said Dan. "You can take work at night school and I have a fine library at my room. I'd be only too glad to lend you some of my books and suggest reading material that will help you. You'll have to hit the line hard, Tim, but you've got the stuff to do it. And besides, Carson likes you and when he knows you are trying to better yourself it will make a big difference with him."

Tim's face was aglow with new hope and courage. "I'll work hard," he promised. "I love the flying game; it's becoming life itself to me and I want to keep on but I won't be satisfied unless I'm something more than a flying reporter."

"I admire your ambition, but don't be too impatient now, Tim," counselled the copyreader. "As a matter of fact you've gone a lot further than most young fellows your age."

"The growth of aviation is going to be like the growth of the newspapers. The young fellows who had plenty of foresight back in 1890 and 1900 are the big men of today. I started in the print shop back in the home town, sweeping out and sorting lead slugs. Got fifty cents a week and thought it was big pay. Next thing, I was setting type by hand out of a case. Used to sit on a high stool from 7 o'clock in the morning until night and the day before we went to press we used to work half the night." Dan smiled a little at the thoughts of the old days.

"When we first read about Mergenthaler and his typesetting machine, we thought he was a nut of some kind. But a few believed in him and today they are the leaders in the newspaper business."

"We used to print our weekly paper on a Washington hand press, and it took us all day to get out a few hundred copies. Now even the weeklies have modern presses while the dailies turn out 36, 48 and 56 page papers by the thousands every hour."

"The same revolution has taken place in the editorial rooms. When I first came to work on the News we had one dinky little telegraph wire that brought only a few hundred words of news a day. We'd take that and pad it out and also used the scissors liberally to cut dispatches out of the big eastern papers. We never knew from one week to another whether our pay checks were good and it was always a race to see who could get to the bank first."

Dan paused for a moment, then he continued, "But look at the office today. A dozen reporters, an editor to handle every department, half a dozen telegraph wires that bring the news from every corner of the world and even an airplane to ferret out the stories in the clouds."

Tim smiled at the last phrase.

"The aviation game is like a newspaper," went on the copyreader. "The newspaper went through its baby days and has emerged into one of the greatest institutions of our modern times. So it will be with aviation. I scoffed at the first strides of modern journalism, and look where I am." There was no note of self-pity in the words, simply a plain statement of fact, and Dan hurried on before Tim could speak.

"I'm only a copyreader while if I had been alert to realize the possibilities way back in the nineties, I might have been the head of this paper or some other like it. I don't want you to miss your chance Tim. You're alert and eager now; keep on that way and I'll help you all I can."

When Tim left the office that afternoon the rain was still falling steadily but he did not feel depressed. He was fired with new enthusiasm and determination. Far into the night he mulled over Dan Watkins' words and he knew that the older man's advice was sound and true. It was a goal Tim had hardly dared dream to attain and one that at times had made his heart ache at the futility of his dreams. But the kindly counsel of the older man had set his mind into new channels of thought and given him the impetus he needed. It was a long, hard road to follow but before he went to sleep, Tim had determined to throw his every energy toward attainment of his goal.

When Tim reached the office the next morning he found Ralph Parsons waiting for him, a camera on his desk.

"Hurry up, Tim," called his chum. "Carson just phoned down and ordered us out on an assignment. They say that the Cedar River is flooding the entire country over east. Worst high water in twenty-five years, and he wants some good pictures for this afternoon's editions. We'll have to hustle."

While Ralph was talking, Tim telephoned to the airport and ordered the Lark serviced and put on the line ready to go. It was raining hard but the weather bulletin indicated clearing weather by mid-forenoon so they would have a chance to get some good pictures when they reached the valley.

Tim and Ralph skidded through the city in one of the News' cars and when they reached the airport found the Lark ready for them, its motor turning over slowly.

Hunter came out of his office.

"It's a bad morning for a takeoff," he warned Tim. "What in thunder is bringing you out on a day like this?"

"We've got a report of a big flood in the Cedar River valley," said Tim, "and Ralph's going to try for some pictures if the rain clears up."

Hunter grunted, then said, "Better keep over to the north side of the field, Tim, and get her off as quick as you can. The other end of this flat is under a good foot of water and it's all pretty much of a swamp."

Tim and Ralph waved at the manager of the field, Tim gave the Lark full throttle, and they sloshed over the field and got away to a sluggish takeoff. The muck and water sucked at the Lark's wheels and it was with an effort that Tim got his craft into the air.

Once clear of the field, he headed into the east. The ceiling was low that morning; not over 500 feet, and the Lark thundered over farms and small towns at better than 100 miles an hour. Tim piloted wholly by compass but after forty-five minutes of flying they ran out of the rain and the sky began to clear. When they sighted the Cedar River valley the sun was out from behind the clouds for the first time in days.

A scene of majestic destruction unfolded itself as Tim swung the Lark over the valley of the Cedar. The usually peaceful stream was on a mighty rampage, its banks hidden by swirling torrents of dirty, yellow water which spread for more than a mile in either direction. In the heart of the foaming flood could be seen great trees, torn up by their roots, and farm buildings that bobbled and turned as if in protest. Over all there was an air of utter desolation, the surrender of man to the wrath of the elements.

Tim was fascinated by the terrible splendor of the scene, and he banked the Lark gracefully as Ralph took picture after picture of the great flood. To the south Tim sighted a cluster of buildings marooned in the center of the raging stream. He turned the plane and sped toward them. In another minute he recognized the village of Auburn, the scene of his first exploit as a flying reporter. The once peaceful hamlet, which, he remembered, had been on the right bank of the Cedar, was surrounded by the rampant waters. While Tim circled the village, Ralph managed to secure two graphic pictures of the marooned village.

Tim could see a little group gathered in front of the general store and once he thought they were gesturing to him, but he dared not go closer. Motor trouble at any lower altitude would mean a plunge into the flood.

A few minutes before noon Tim dropped the crimson-winged Lark down out of the clouds and skidded over the muddy field. He uncurled his legs and got stiffly out of the cockpit. Ralph hopped down beside him, his camera under his arm.

They left orders for mechanics at the field to take care of the plane and then headed toward the city in the car they had left at the field.

"That's some flood," said Ralph as they sped toward the office. "I didn't think there was so much water in the whole world."

Tim was preoccupied and his words were slow in coming.

"I'm wondering how things are at Auburn," said he. "With communication cut off, they might be in bad shape. Wish we could have gone lower but I didn't dare, and we had to get your plates back as soon as possible."

When they entered the editorial office, the managing editor was waiting for them.

"Get 'em?" he demanded.

"You bet," said Ralph, "some dandies," and he laid his camera with its graphic record of the flood, on the managing editor's desk.

Carson hurriedly made out a rush order for the engraving room and sent a copy boy scurrying away with the camera. In less than an hour they would appear on the front page of the noonday extra, a real scoop over every other paper in town.

When Tim and Ralph went out for lunch, the sky was overcast again with hurrying rain clouds and the city was shrouded in a pall of low-lying clouds and heavy smoke. They were gone not more than half an hour but when they returned Carson beckoned at them, one ear glued to a telephone receiver. He was writing rapidly, occasionally asking a tense question. When he had finished he turned to Tim.

"This is bad, Tim," said the managing editor. "That little town of Auburn that you flew over this morning had been isolated for four days now. They're getting low on food and typhoid has broken out in the village. There isn't a boat left in the village and even if trucks could get near there with boats, the river is so churned up they wouldn't be able to get out to the village. I've just talked to the owner of the general store at Auburn. He'd taken to a barn door and trusted to luck that the current would take him ashore. He got through safely and called us from Applington. They're appealing to us to do something."

"Get me the food and serum they need and I'll drop it to them in less than two hours," replied Tim rising to the challenge in the managing editor's eyes.

CHAPTER FIVE

Tim's instant response to the appeal from the flood-stricken village pleased the managing editor immensely.

"Fine, Tim, fine," said Carson. "This will be great stuff. Good advertising for the News and at the same time a real bit of service. I'll call the Red Cross and have everything ready. How much can you carry?"

"About five hundred pounds," said the flying reporter. "Have them put it in two strong sacks, big ones, and get it to the field in half an hour. I'll hustle out there and get a parachute ready."

"Where do I come in?" expostulated Ralph, who had no intention of being left out of the party. "If you're going to take five hundred pounds of food and medical supplies, there won't be room for me."

"I know it, Ralph, and I'm sorry," replied Tim. "But right now the food and medicine mean more to those villagers than your presence circling around in the clouds above them."

Tim's words were without sarcasm and Ralph grinned in spite of his disappointment, but he knew that Tim was right.

"I'll go out to the field with you," he volunteered, "and I may be able to help you fix the parachute."

"You could help a lot," agreed Tim, and they hurried out of the office on their way to the airport.

When they reached the field, Tim enlisted the aid of Hunter and they opened up a parachute pack. Springs were carefully inserted and so arranged that they would force the big silken umbrella open three seconds after it had been dropped from the plane.

They were just completing their work with the parachute when a truck from the Red Cross office arrived with the supplies, packed in two strong canvas sacks.

"The serum's in the center of one of the bags," said the truck driver, "and they said you wouldn't need to worry about breaking the glass tubes. They've packed everything carefully."

Tim soon rigged the sacks on the side of the Lark with the parachute attached to them. A single hard jerk on the rope which held the sacks would send them tumbling earthward to the stricken village.

The flying reporter checked his plane with even greater care than usual. He couldn't afford to take a risk, too much depended on the outcome of his flight. Finally, satisfied that all was well, he climbed into the rear cockpit and settled his long legs on the rudder bar. The motor was purring musically.

Ralph climbed up on the fuselage and bent close to Tim, "Good luck," he shouted, and slapped his chum on the back.

That was characteristic of the generousness of Ralph's nature and Tim warmed inwardly for he knew how keenly Ralph wanted to make the trip with him.

With a roar of the motor and a flirt of its tail, Tim sent the Lark rocketing into the eastern sky on its errand of mercy while the great presses in the News building uptown were even then grinding out the story of his daring attempt.

After a little less than an hour of flying, he sighted the swirling, dirty-yellow current of the Cedar and swung down the valley to pick up the marooned village, a cluster of houses in the midst of a great expanse of angry flood waters.

The roar of the Lark's motor attracted the attention of the villagers and they gathered in the town square to watch the circling plane. Tim swept low and pointed to the sacks on the side of his plane. The expressions on the upturned faces of the people indicated that they understood what he was going to attempt.

Tim banked sharply and headed upstream. The clouds had broken somewhat but there were indications of an almost momentary squall. He would have to hurry to accomplish his mission. The winds were hard out of the east and it would take careful calculations of speed and wind drift to land his cargo on the tiny island.

When he was a mile upstream from the village, Tim turned and headed down stream, ready for the attempt. He cut the speed of the Lark as low as he dared and waited until he judged the right moment was at hand. Then he jerked the rope that held his precious cargo to the side of the plane. He saw the sacks drop away and watched the parachute spring open and billow out in the breeze.

For a moment Tim watched the parachute falling straight and true. The wind was a trifle stronger than he had anticipated but it looked as if the sacks would land near the far end of the island.

A sudden squall swept over the valley and rain blotted out the scene below. It was over in thirty seconds but when Tim sighted the parachute again it was settling into the churning waters at the south end of the island. The villagers desperately cast long poles with hooked ends into the stream in an effort to snare the parachute and pull it to shore, but in less than a minute the silken umbrella, with its two sacks of serum and food, were sucked down by the hungry Cedar.

Tim was heart-sick when he turned the Lark up-stream, nosed down, and sped over the village again. He leaned over the side of the cockpit and tried, with gestures, to tell the disappointed group that he would return to Atkinson, secure more supplies, and make another attempt. But in his heart he doubted if the second trip would be any more successful than the first. The clouds were heavier and the winds had increased to almost gale strength. Riding on the wings of the easterly wind, he swept down on the Atkinson airport just forty minutes after his unsuccessful attempt to relieve the suffering at Auburn.

While his plane splashed over the muddy field and slithered to a stop in front of the office, Tim evolved a plan which might mean the salvation of the villagers. Desperate it was, and its chances of success would be slim, but it was worth trying if he could convince his managing editor.

Carson was at the field waiting for news of the flight. At his side was Ralph Parsons, a camera in hand.

"Just a minute, Tim," yelled the managing editor, as the young flyer started to climb down from him mud-bespattered plane.

"Pose in your ship while we get some pictures of the 'Hero of the Air.'"

Tim shook his head. "Not now Mr. Carson, I'm anything but a hero. I failed."

"What," exclaimed the managing editor, for failure was something that so far had not entered into the life of the flying reporter. "Why what do you mean, Tim?"

"The sacks landed in the river," explained Tim. "I had them aimed all right but a little squall swept over the valley after I released them and carried them too far."

Carson was silent and his disappointment was evident. Then Tim went on.

"But Mr. Carson, if ever any group of people needs help, that little town of Auburn does. I went down so close I could see their faces; they're desperate. Give me another chance and I'll make good."

"There isn't time today," said the managing editor.

"Yes there is, if we work fast."

"Won't the same thing happen again?"

"No!" There was ringing conviction in Tim's words. "I'll get the stuff there or bust in the attempt. Besides, I've got a new plan."

Carson looked at his flying reporter for a moment. The light in Tim's blue eyes and the determined lines around his mouth convinced the managing editor that he could back up his words with success.

"All right," he agreed, "shoot."

For a minute Tim and the managing editor, with Ralph listening in, talked earnestly.

"I think you're crazy," exclaimed Carson, "But it's worth a try. It's your neck; not mine that you're risking." With that the managing editor hurried to his car and sped toward the city to fulfill his part of the preparations.

"Do you think you can do it?" Ralph anxiously wanted to know as they hurried toward the main office of the airport.

"There isn't any 'think' about it, Ralph," replied Tim. "I've got to. This is going to cost the News some good, hard cash and if I fall down on this job I won't need to come back. And you know what that would mean to me."

Ralph was silent, weighing his chum's chances for success, and they talked no more until they reached the office and entered the manager's room.

Hunter looked up from his desk.

"Make it?" he asked.

"No such luck, Carl," said Tim. "The wind blew it into the river."

"Say, that's too bad," said the field manager. "I guess those folks over in the valley are in bad shape, too."

"They need help," agreed Tim, "and I'm going to make another try right away. Is that old Jenny over in hangar No. 3 capable of staggering into the air?"

"You mean the sister to the ship Ralph cracked up a few weeks ago?"

"That's the one."

"It might get off the ground but I wouldn't guarantee it would stay in the air. What do you want with that old crate?"

"Never mind that, Carl. How much do you want for it if we can get the motor to turn over fast enough to get into the air?"

Hunter whistled and scratched his ear reflectively. "About $200 the way she is, but I won't promise a thing. You'll have to take your chances."

"Sold!" said Tim, "Carson said I could buy that war relic providing you didn't try to hold me up. He'll O.K. the bill when he comes back. Let's get going."

With Ralph and Hunter at his heels, he hurried toward hangar No. 3. There, in one corner of the big structure, was a venerable Jenny, a sister ship to the one Ralph had smashed on his first solo hop. Orders flew from Tim and Hunter and in less than fifteen minutes a crew of mechanics had gone over the old plane, filled its motor with gas and oil, and had it warming up in front of the hangar.

"Got any old canvas around?" Tim asked Hunter.

"There's some in No. 2 hangar. How much do you need?"

"Just enough to cover the bottom of the fuselage of this ancient sky bird and make it water proof," said Tim. Hunter hustled out to find the heavy fabric while Ralph hurried away in quest of a pot of shellac.

By the time the managing editor returned from the city with a new supply of serum and food, the Jenny was a queer looking bird. The bottom of the fuselage had been covered with heavy canvas and doused liberally with quick drying shellac to make it water-tight. The decrepit wings showed where new patches had been hurriedly slapped on and mechanics had completed emergency wiring of the wings to insure them from collapsing and sending Tim spinning down from the clouds with his plane out of control.

The new sacks of supplies were dumped into the forward cockpit. Tim swung into the rear pit, ran the throttle back and forth and listened to the song of the motor. Its r.p.m.'s were a little slow but it was firing steady and true. He waggled the controls to be sure that everything responded and then slipped his goggles down over his eyes.

"Don't take too many chances," the managing editor yelled as he revved up the motor.

Tim waved his hand, and then pushed the throttle on full. The old skybird quivered and gathered herself for the takeoff. The wings creaked and groaned but the motor responded to its task and Tim finally lifted the old crate off the ground and soared into the east for the third time that day.

He glanced at his wrist watch. It was nearly 5 o'clock and that meant only a little more than an hour of light left in which to accomplish his task. With 100 miles to the valley and against the wind all the way, it required nearly an hour and a half for the old ship couldn't turn a mile over eighty an hour.

Tim settled down to do some straight and careful flying. He nursed the old crate along for all it was worth and the "Hisso" hammered until he thought it would throw connecting rods all over the countryside.

For nearly an hour Tim dodged rain squalls. Then, realizing that he was getting down into the river territory, he brought the old crate closer to the ground.

As he sped along above the broken landscape, Tim craned from the cockpit, watching the ground below with eyes that smarted in the sharp backwash of the propeller.

When he found a large field, fenced in with heavy posts, he banked sharply and dropped his plane closer to the ground. Now he was roaring along not more than ten feet above the soggy, waterlogged field. It was anything but an inviting spot for a forced landing. As a matter of fact Tim knew he wouldn't have a chance for any kind of a landing if his motor cut out on him then.

Ahead of him loomed the edge of the field with its fence. He picked out one post, which reared its head higher than the others. The flying reporter, like Don Quixote of old who had sent his horse galloping into a windmill, headed his craft for the sturdy timber.

The big test was at hand. It would require all the skill in Tim's hands and all his nerve to accomplish it successfully. A false move and the Jenny would be a heap on the ground, his chance of relieving the situation at Auburn gone for he had staked everything, even his job, on this attempt.

Just before the propeller ripped into the post Tim pulled back hard on the stick. The Jenny answered sluggishly and his heart skipped a beat. The plane staggered in midair and Tim heard the sound of rending wood. Then the old craft lunged on and upward, shaking herself like an injured bird. Tim looked back to see his landing gear draped over the post.

He could hardly repress a shout as he headed the old crate for the valley again. In the air, the Jenny looked like a flying washboard but Tim had accomplished one part of his task. He had converted his craft into a seaplane of sorts. True it was that in design and balance it violated every rule of aeronautics, but it flew and that was the big thing. Now to land safely on the river.

When Tim reached the valley the rain was falling in torrents and the clouds seemed to be crushing him to earth. The light was nearly gone and he would have to work fast.

The old crate was vibrating more than ever. The crash into the post must have loosened something in the vitals of the Jenny for it was obviously near the end of its long career. If it would only hold together a few more minutes it would wind up its life in a smashing climax.

The tired old "Hisso" sputtered, then caught again and fired steadily. But Tim knew the signs. The rain was finding its way through the cowling and down onto the motor. It would be only a matter of minutes before the motor would cut out. Now it was a race between the coming night, a weakening motor and the flood-maddened Cedar. The odds were great but Tim faced them coolly.

He roared over the village and swept upstream. Then he turned and came down low over the river. A quarter of a mile above the upper end of the island he was barely skimming the surface of the river. He cut the motor, there was plenty of speed left.

Then Tim set his flying scow down on the water. He struck with a crash, bounced, struck again, and splashed along on top of the foaming water. He was going fast, too fast for comfort, but there was nothing he could do. The island loomed ahead. Tim shut his eyes and ducked behind the cockpit. There was a sickening lurch, then a jarring thud that shook the whole plane.

Anxious hands pulled Tim out of the cockpit while others seized the sacks of food and medical supplies. A tree stump had broken the speed of the plane but it had struck the bank hard enough to smash the propeller to bits and bury the nose of the engine in the dirt.

Later in the evening, after the village doctor had made good use of the typhoid serum and the food had been rationed out, Tim made his way back to the scene of his landing.

The hungry Cedar had been tugging at the wrecked plane and, as Tim reached the river's edge, it swung the craft away from the bank and out into the current. The old crate was gone but it had had a glorious finish. He would have a great story to send to the News as soon as boats were able to reach the village.

CHAPTER SIX

Several days after his flight with supplies to the marooned village in the Cedar river valley, Tim had an unexpected visitor. He looked up from his work to find a tall, curly haired man of not more than thirty years of age, standing beside his desk.

"Are you Tim Murphy?" inquired the visitor. Tim nodded.

"I'm Kurt Blandin, boss of the Ace flying circus," replied the other. "I hear one of the boys treated you rather roughly the other day and I thought I'd drop in and invite you to come and see us again."

Tim thought he noted a peculiar, strained quality in the other's voice, and he deliberated his answer.

"I'll run out some day," he said. "As a matter of fact I couldn't see any reason why I was given the cold shoulder when I was out the first time."

Blandin laughed and Tim found himself rather liking the other when he smiled.

"An air circus," he said, "is bound to have some accidents and sometimes we aren't treated any too well in the newspapers. So you can't blame the mechanic for giving you the bum's rush. But everything will be O. K. the next time you call." With that Blandin breezed out of the office and Tim stared after him blankly.

Somewhere he had seen the face before. There were familiar lines about the mouth, a peculiar little scar over the right eye and a hardness of the voice that once heard would never be forgotten.

He forced his thoughts back to his work but Blandin and the Ace air circus troubled him. What were they doing at Atkinson? Could there be any connection between them and the Sky Hawk?

The ghostly quiet that comes just before the dawn was broken by the insistent voice of the telephone.

Tim rubbed the sleep from his eyes and grabbed savagely at the offending instrument.

"Hello, hello!" he barked.

An anxious voice came over the wire.

"What!" Tim's exclamation was charged with alarm. "You're sure? All right, I'll be at the field just as soon as I can throw on some clothes and get in touch with Ralph."

Tim jammed the receiver on its hook, only to seize it a moment later and something in his voice made the operator buzz furiously as she rang Ralph's number. After an interval that seemed an age to Tim, a sleepy voice answered the operator's imperative rings.

"That you, Ralph?" cried Tim. When the voice admitted that it belonged to Ralph, Tim poured his story over the wire.

"Wake up, Ralph. Wake up," he urged. "There's plenty of trouble over in the Big Smokies. Bad Storm last night and the west-bound Transcontinental plane has crashed somewhere. They haven't had a trace of it since the ship went over Newton. The Transcontinental people have sent out a general alarm and Hunter just phoned and asked us to help in the search. Meet me at the field just as soon as you can get there."

Ralph, thoroughly awakened by Tim's words, promised to be at the field in fifteen minutes.

The flying reporter completed dressing and hastened from his room in quest of a taxicab. A driver, on the lookout for early morning fares, was loafing down the street and Tim hailed the cab.

"To the municipal field," he ordered when the cab pulled up at the curb, "and step on the gas. This is important."

The gears crashed together and the cab lurched away into the night, gathering speed as it headed down the almost deserted avenues.

When they reached the field they found it ablaze with light. Pilots and mechanics were hurrying in and out of the hangars and planes were being warmed up and pushed on the line.

"Charge it to the News," said Tim as he disembarked. Hunter, who came running out of the office, greeted him.

"Glad to see you, Tim," he said. "We're getting things lined up to start as soon as it gets light. I've put a crew to servicing your plane and she'll be ready in a few minutes. Where's Ralph? Isn't he going?"

Hunter's question was answered by another snorting taxi, and Ralph, only half awake, tumbled from the car.

"What's all the excitement and the big rush to get away so quick?" demanded Tim. "The air mail has cracked up before and has always come out on top."

"Plenty of reason for the rush this time," said Hunter. "The plane last night was carrying something like $500,000 in securities from New York for a Los Angeles bank."

Tim whistled. "No wonder they're getting everything out that can flap its wings. We'll be with the rest of them, Carl, and glad of the chance to go. It will make a dandy story."

Tim did not voice his real thoughts for there was no need to unduly alarm the field manager, but the minute the $500,000 had been mentioned, the thought of the Sky Hawk flashed through his mind. It was about time for that daring bandit of the skyways to swoop down in some bold manoeuvre. The storm might have been responsible for the failure of the mail to reach its destination and, again, it might not.

"Called you right away," added the field manager, "for I knew you'd want the story. But on top of that, I wanted you to make the trip. I figure you're one of the best pilots around here to go out on a mission like this."

Tim grinned and gave Hunter a good-natured shove. The driver of Ralph's taxi was turning his cab around and preparing to start back for the city when Tim's cry stopped him.

"Wait a few minutes," he ordered, "and I'll have you take a story to the News office." The driver agreed and shut off the motor of his cab.

"Check up on the plane, Ralph," said Tim, "and see that we have plenty of equipment for an emergency landing in the mountains—light, stout cable, an axe, some food and water and a first aid kit. While you're doing that I'll go into Hunter's room and write a story to send to the office."

In less than fifteen minutes Tim had hammered out a column story that fairly glittered with the sharpness of its sentences and the clearness of his simple, powerful English.

The air mail was lost somewhere in the Great Smokies, and the flying reporter, in the Lark, would soon be away on the search. Tim smiled to himself as he thought how Carson could play up the story. Now if they could only find the missing plane, it would be one of the best stories of the year.

Tim hurried out of the office and handed his story to the waiting taxi driver. That done, he turned toward the line where five planes were being warmed up for the search.

The flying reporter walked over to the airmen who were grouped around the field manager. He greeted Sparks, Bronson, White and Wilkins, all mail and express pilots—fine fellows every one of them; lean bronzed and alive to the zest of flying. But now there were more serious lines to their faces and it was a determined group of young men who heard Hunter outline the plans for the search. Ralph hastened up and joined them just as the field chief gave his final instructions.

"Buddy Perkins, who was on the mail, went over Newton on time," said Hunter, "and he must have run into the storm about half an hour later. That would put him almost up to the divide but with the wind against him all the way, he probably didn't make Billy Goat. I've marked out a map with the section each one of you is to cover. When you run short of fuel about noon, drop down to Newton, refuel, eat and exchange notes. I hope you won't have to go on out again, hope you'll locate Perkins by noon. It's light enough to takeoff now, fellows, so get going and good luck."

Tim and Ralph took their places in the Good News, which was the third ship on the line. It was just light enough to distinguish the fence which marked the far end of the field.

Sparks and Bronson roared away, flame shooting from the exhausts of their motors. Then Tim shoved his throttle ahead and sent the Lark skimming into the air. Behind him came White and Wilkins. Away into the west they sped, traveling on the wings of the dawn, intent on their quest for the missing Perkins.

Within the hour they had roared over Newton, nestled in the foothills of the Great Smokies, and had started clawing for altitude. The Lark handled beautifully in the cool air of the early September morning and answered to Tim's every movement.

The flying reporter could see Sparks and Bronson swing away to his left while White and Wilkins turned to the right to cover the territory which Hunter had mapped out for each plane. Tim was more fortunate than the other flyers for he had Ralph's keen eyes to help him comb the uneven ground below. Ahead of them loomed the Billy Goat, the highest peak of the range. Tim's sector was on the east slope of the lofty mountain. Up and down, back and forth, Tim swung the Lark as he shuttled along the path usually followed by the air mail and express planes. The Billy Goat glistened in the morning sun but smiled grimly—almost defiantly Tim imagined, as it thwarted his every effort to find any trace of the missing plane.

By mid-forenoon Tim's gas supply was getting low and he signalled to Ralph that he was going to turn back to Newton and replenish his fuel. They were near the top of Billy Goat and both Tim and Ralph felt certain that if Perkins had crashed on that side of the mountain they would have sighted him.

Tim cut his motor and let the Lark soar gracefully downward from the summit of the range. For a moment he forgot the urgent mission which had brought them out and reveled in the sheer joy of flying. Like a great bird his plane wheeled and swooped in the sky.

Half way to Newton Tim was joined by Sparks and White. They landed at the emergency field at the foothill town and a few minutes later were joined by Bronson and Wilkins. There was no need to ask about their success. Their faces told the story of the failure of their efforts.

While the other pilots were refueling their planes, Tim hurried into the village where he secured a basket of sandwiches. He made several inquiries in the village and related the result of these when he returned to the field.

The airmen sprawled beneath their planes and hastily munched the sandwiches Tim had provided.

"You say he went through here on time?" asked White, who had been a close friend of the missing Perkins.

"That's what they say in Newton," replied Tim. "The storm was threatening when Perk went over and he was flying pretty low and fast. About half an hour after he passed, the storm swept down from Billy Goat and from what folks here say, it was a bad one."

"Half an hour," grunted Ralph between bites of a sandwich. "That means he was pretty well up toward the divide. Maybe he got across on the other side."

"It's just too bad if he did," remarked Bronson. "You know what the other side of the Billy Goat is like. Not a nickel's worth of room for a forced landing. If Perk got on the other side he's crashed sure."

"Might not be that bad," said Tim. "Anyway, I'm going to try the other side of Billy Goat this afternoon."

"Look out you don't disappear along with Perk," warned White.

"Not much chance of that with Ralph along," grinned Tim. "I'll see you fellows here later."

The foothills awoke to the roar of five high-powered airplane motors and one after another the flyers took off to resume their hunt.

Tim gunned the Lark and headed straight for the crest of the Great Smokies. The divide was a little to the right of Billy Goat. Tim boosted his plane over the snow-capped tops of the range and coasted down the other side. The slope on the west side was more broken—deep canyons with good-sized streams plunging along in their depths. But from the plane the rivers looked like ribbons of silver. It was a scene of majestic beauty but it gave Tim the shivers when he thought of being trapped on the inhospitable slope in a storm or, worse, at the mercy of the Sky Hawk.

For fifty miles Tim and Ralph followed the path of the mail and express ships, searching every valley, but their efforts were fruitless.

Tim frowned bitterly and turned the Lark eastward in a tight bank. Ralph looked back apprehensively but Tim only shook his head and pointed southeast. How blind he had been. If Perkins had made the crest of the divide and gotten over before the storm caught him, he would probably have been driven southwest along the side of the mountains. The Great Smokies ran northeast and southwest and the storm of the night before had swept down almost directly from the north.

When Tim again reached the western slope of the Billy Goat, he headed south and west. He scribbled a note to Ralph, explaining his reason for the sudden about face, and his companion nodded approval.

For an hour they searched the side of the range south of Billy Goat, and Tim, with an eye on the gas gauge, was about to give up the quest, when Ralph shouted and pointed downward.

A flash of white on a rocky ledge caught Tim's eye and he circled lower. His breath caught sharply. Ralph's sharp eyes had found the wreck of the air express. On a ledge of rock cropping out from the side of the mountain they could see the twisted remains of the plane!

CHAPTER SEVEN

Tim stalled down over the wreck of the air mail. There was no sign of life; no sign of Perk. His heart caught in his throat. Perk had been a mighty good flyer and a good fellow. Tim bad known him only casually but he had been well liked by all the other pilots in the air service. There was a chance that the airman, unharmed in the crackup, might have started to make his way out of the wilderness of broken rock and tangled forest on foot.

Tim made a careful survey of the shelf that jutted out from the mountain side. It was not more than 100 feet wide and perhaps 400 feet long—a dangerous place on which to attempt a landing.

The flying reporter shut off his motor.

"What do you say?" he shouted at Ralph, and pointed to the ledge.

"Go on," came the reply. "You'll make it all right."

Tim tore off his goggles and Ralph did likewise. No use endangering their eyes if they crashed.

The flying reporter put the Lark into a sideslip. Just before they slid into the side of the mountain he leveled off and set the plane down almost on the edge of the rocky shelf. The ship bounded forward and he shoved the brakes on hard. They were still going fast, too fast. In a few more seconds they would pile up on the rocks ahead. Tim jammed his left wheel brake on hard and released the right one. The plane staggered, dug its left wing into the ground and almost did a ground loop. But the maneuver killed the speed and Ralph and Tim leaped from their plane and ran toward the wreck of the air mail.

From the looks of things, Perkins, blinded by the storm and driven far off his course, had rammed straight into the side of the mountain. The nose of the big biplane, with the motor, had been bashed back into the express cockpit and the landing gear had folded up.

Tim fairly leaped up the side of the fuselage and into the pilot's cockpit, but Perkins was nowhere in sight. On the padded leather seat Tim found a folded sheet of paper. With eager fingers he grasped it and read its message at a glance.

"Hello, Tim," he read. "The first time we met you won; this time fate brought the mail into my hands and right now I'm richer by some $500,000, which will keep me out of mischief for some time. I just happened to be crossing the Great Smokies this morning and saw the mail, which had cracked up in the storm last night. Don't you wish you had a helicopter on your plane to lift you off this ledge? But I don't think the pilot is badly hurt. See you later, and remember, the score is even."

There was no need for Tim to read the name signed to the note. The Sky Hawk, profiting by the vagaries of the storm, had struck again!

Ralph, who had gone around to the far side of the plane, cried out. When Tim reached his chum he found him under one wing, bending over the unconscious form of the mail pilot.

There was a jagged cut on one side of Perkins' head where he must have come in contact with some part of the plane in the crackup. His face was a grayish-white and Tim instantly realized that he was in need of expert medical attention.

"How badly do you think he's hurt?" asked Ralph.

"I don't know," replied Tim. "He's got a nasty crack on the head and it may be serious and it may not. Get me the first aid kit in our ship and I'll dress this wound on his head."

In less than five minutes Tim had dressed the cut and with Ralph's assistance, had carried Perkins into the sunlight where his clothes, still damp from the rain of the night before, would have a chance to dry. He was breathing slowly but regularly and they forced a little water between his lips. While they were working over Perk, Tim showed the Sky Hawk's note to Ralph, and their lips were drawn in hard, straight lines as they realized the power of the unknown bandit of the skyways.

Both Tim and Ralph knew that their real task, that of making a successful takeoff from the narrow ledge, was their biggest problem and they turned to it with determination. With Perkins taken care of temporarily, they made sure that the remaining registered mail was O. K. and then transferred it to their own plane. After that they started their survey of the shelf on which they had landed. On one side was the mountain, on the other a drop of nearly 1,000 feet. The surface of the shelf was fairly even but it was only about 400 feet long, far too short for a takeoff, especially with three in the Lark as there would be on the return trip.

"Looks like we're going to be marooned here along with Perk," said Ralph dubiously.

"It isn't quite as bad as all that," replied Tim. "If you're willing to take a long chance, I think we can make it."

"What do you mean?"

"You've seen those pictures of how the navy uses a catapult to launch its fighting planes from the decks of battleships?" Ralph nodded.

"We'll use the same principle. Shoot ourselves into the air."

"But we haven't any catapult and the nearest battleship is a thousand miles away," said Ralph, still unconvinced.

"All right," said Tim. "I'll show you how it can be done. Give me a hand now."

Under Tim's directions, they managed to trundle the Lark to the end of the ledge where the air mail had crashed. There they turned it around and pointed its nose toward the far end of the shelf.

"What now?" demanded Ralph.

"Open up that bundle of light cable we brought and get out the axe," said Tim.

When that had been completed he took the cable and tied one end securely around a huge boulder directly back of the tail assembly of the Lark. The other end he passed along the fuselage and lashed around the nose of the ship.

"Simple, isn't it?" asked Tim when he had made sure that the ends of the cable had been properly secured.

"Simple, yes," agreed Ralph. "But what does it spell?"

"C-a-t-a-p-u-l-t," said Tim. "C-a-t-a-p-u-l-t."

"I heard you the first time, but that doesn't look like a catapult to me."

"Well, it is," insisted Tim. "And if you'll stop asking questions and help me boost Perkins into your cockpit, we'll get out of here. It's getting late now and will be dark by the time we get to Atkinson."

Together they managed to get the inert form of Perkins into the forward cockpit and made him as comfortable as possible. Tim primed the starter and the motor caught on the first turn over.

Ralph was looking skeptically at Tim's make-shift catapult.

"When I give her full throttle you slash the rope with the axe," explained Tim. "I'll admit that isn't much of a catapult but it will give us a lot of added momentum when you use the axe." Ralph, only half convinced, hopped into his cockpit and leaned over the side, axe in hand.

Tim tested the sturdy motor thoroughly. If it failed him when he started on his mad takeoff, they would plunge 1,000 feet down the side of the mountain to be impaled on the tall pines far below.

Satisfied that the motor would do its share, Tim settled himself for the test. He glanced ahead. The edge of the shelf looked dangerously near but there was no other course to take. He must get Perkins where he could have the best of medical attention.

Tim opened his throttle. Faster and faster he threw the raw gas into the motor until the plane quivered like a thing alive. The engine was thrumming wildly and Tim threw up his left hand, the signal for Ralph to cut the cable.

With a well-aimed blow, Ralph's axe bit through the rope and the Lark leaped forward like an arrow and flashed toward the edge of the precipice.

The plane bounced from side to side on the uneven ground and Tim held his breath as they swooped nearer the end of their short runway. But the plane was gaining speed rapidly. How rapidly, he didn't dare look.

At the last moment Tim pulled back hard on the stick but it was as though some giant had tied a string to the Lark and was playing with them. The plane staggered into the air, settled back, bounced hard, and then shot skyward. They were off at last but hovering dizzily in the air. The motor labored at its task and Tim sensed a losing battle. The added weight of Perkins in the front cockpit might be just enough to turn the scales against them. In another second they would be in a spin, hurtling down to death on the gaunt pines.

In a flash Tim took his only chance and threw the Lark into a power dive. That would give him the momentum necessary to handle his craft. Down the side of the mountain roared the plane, the wild beating of its motor echoing and re-echoing among the cliffs and valleys. They were almost on the tree tops when Tim pulled the nose of his ship up and leveled off with his plane under control.

Tim set his course for the crest of the range and was just sliding around the Billy Goat when the sun went down in the west, a great, red ball of fire. The evening shadows were thickening, for night comes quickly in the mountains.

The Lark made splendid time and they were less than fifty miles from Atkinson when Tim sighted the gray bank of fog rolling out of the east. Although fogs were not uncommon at that time of year he had not counted on that hazard.

With his gas getting low there was only one thing to do—hammer through and trust to his compass to bring him over his home field.

The cold, gray banks swallowed the little plane and Tim was flying in a world alone. The mist was so thick that Ralph, only a half dozen feet ahead of him, was only a blurred outline.

On all sides the fog mocked the flying reporter but he was determined to get through. A glance at the gas gauge was none too reassuring. His fuel was running low but if his calculations were correct, there would be enough to finish his task.

Tim turned on the light on his instrument board for it was quite dark by that time. He penciled a note to Ralph, asking him how Perkins was standing the trip. Then Tim took a wrench and tapped on the fuselage to attract Ralph's attention.

Ralph leaned back and Tim handed him the message. Two or three minutes later they repeated the operation, this time transferring a note from Ralph to Tim. The flying reporter read his chum's hasty scrawl.

"Perk's all right so far but mighty white and quiet. Do you know where you are?"

Tim had to admit that he wasn't exactly sure of their location but he kept on hoping for the best.

When Tim figured that he must be almost over Atkinson, he dropped as low as he dared, a careful eye on the altimeter, while he hunted for a rift in the fog that would allow him to land.

A light spot glowed ahead—perhaps the reflection of the lights of the city. For a moment the fog parted and Tim got a fleeting glimpse of Atkinson. But before he could locate the airport, the city was blotted from view.

Ralph, who had been on the lookout, had seen the lights and now was looking at Tim expectantly.

Tim fumed and raged against the luck of the elements and while he circled over the city his precious supply of fuel trickled away. The motor sputtered and he turned on the emergency tank enough for twenty minutes more of flying. Then they'd have to come down and probably crack-up in the process. It wasn't a nice picture that flashed into his mind. Probably he would be safe enough for his cockpit was well back in the fuselage, but it would be tough on Ralph and the unconscious Perkins. Desperately, Tim searched his mind for some way out; some way to minimize the danger.

He gripped the controls harder as a plan took form. Tim put the Lark into a steep climb and soon reached the 3,000 foot level, plenty high enough for his purpose. Then he signalled for Ralph to crawl back into his cockpit.

Ralph scrambled back over the fuselage and his face, illuminated by the light on the instrument board, showed his amazement at the plan Tim unfolded.

"You can't do that, Tim," he protested. "It's too risky. I won't stand for it. We'll stick by the ship and take our chances."

"Not on your life," replied Tim. "We can't risk Perk's life in a crackup and my plan is the only way out. You take the stick and tend to business. See you later."

With that Tim scrambled into the forward cockpit where he busied himself, making sure that Perkins' head was well bandaged. Then he unsnapped the safety belt, pulled Perkins into an almost vertical position, and lashed the body of the unconscious airman securely to his own.

Tim was glad that Perkins was slight in stature. With a heavier man his plan would have failed. Somehow he managed to work himself up on the edge of the cockpit with Perkins held to him by the safety belt.

Tim looked back at Ralph and waved his hand reassuringly. Then, aided by a mighty shove by his feet, he hurled himself into the fog, pulling Perkins with him. As he fell, Tim thought he heard a shout from Ralph.

Down, down, down they tumbled before Tim could find the ring and jerk his parachute. It was an eternity before he heard the pilot chute crack open to be followed a moment later by a dull sort of an explosion as the big chute unfolded and filled with air. A violent jerk stopped their mad descent and Tim hugged Perkins closer to him.

Maybe he had been foolhardy to desert the ship and trust to the silken umbrella to get them down, but it had seemed the only way to protect Perkins from what was sure to be a crash if they stayed by the plane. Tim figured that they would get nothing more than a hard bump when they landed and he could swing Perkins around and shield him. Ralph was fully capable of taking care of himself and the fortune in securities they had salvaged from the wreck of the air express.

Far away Tim heard the sound of an airplane motor. Probably his own ship. He hoped that the Lark wouldn't be wrecked when Ralph was forced down.

The sound of the motor came nearer. It was the Lark for Tim knew its song by heart. Suddenly his face blanched. Somewhere to his right the plane was roaring down on them through the fog. With Ralph's visibility at zero, it might run into them and chew them to pieces.

Tim strained to one side as he listened to the higher note of the motor. He grasped the shrouds of the parachute, ready to spill the air from the chute in an attempt to escape the plane if it was necessary. The added burden of carrying Perkins was a cruel strain on his body.

The roar of the motor filled the heavens as the Lark flashed out of the fog. Tim cried out in agony and horror for they were directly in the path of the ship. He closed his eyes and pulled the shrouds with every ounce of strength left in his weary body. They dropped earthward quickly as the air spilled from the chute.

But Tim's tired mind had not acted quickly enough. Although they escaped the deadly whirl of the propeller, the tail of the plane took a husky bite at the chute. A great chunk of the strong silk wedged itself into the tail assembly and Tim's body was almost jerked apart as he was pulled upward and after the plane. It couldn't last long; it was more than his body could stand. He screamed under the agony of the awful strain and his eyes stared upward into Ralph's terror-stricken face, as he fought to protect the unconscious Perkins while they were pulled through the sky like the tail of a great rocket.

CHAPTER EIGHT

The burden of the chute slowed the plane. Then it leaped almost vertically as Ralph attempted to free it from the human burden it was dragging through the sky. The whole thing required a second, not more than two, when part of the tail assembly gave way and the chute started its downward course again. It had been an endless span of years to Tim, who sobbed aloud as they drifted through the fog.

Lights pierced the mist below and Tim instinctively swung around to protect Perkins when they landed. But they didn't land. The chute caught in a maze of telephone wires along one of the main highways on the outskirts of Atkinson and Tim and Perkins dangled just above the ground. Passing motorists released them and rushed them to a hospital where Perkins was given immediate attention and Tim was put to bed after a thorough massage to ease his strained muscles. But not until he had telephoned the office and dictated the first part of the story of their finding of the wreck of the air mail and their sensational trip above Atkinson with the injured pilot.

Tim, who had been almost forcibly put in bed by the hospital attendants, was protesting that he had work to do when Ralph burst into the room.

"Are you all right, Tim?" he demanded.

"Sure," replied Tim. "How about yourself and the plane?"

"Both O. K.," said Ralph. "I blew out a couple of tires in landing and broke the prop, but that's all. How's Perk?"

Tim turned to the head surgeon who had just entered the room.

"He'll be back in the air in a few days," said the surgeon. "He has a nasty crack on the head and it was a good thing you got him here when you did. Much more exposure and he would have had pneumonia."

The surgeon had just stepped from the room when the managing editor of the News hurried in.

"Wonderful work, Tim," said Carson. "Wonderful. We put out an extra on the story you phoned. Now let's have the rest of it. This Sky Hawk angle makes it the most thrilling yarn of the year."

For the better part of half an hour, Tim and Ralph related their experiences while a stenographer took down their story.

The next day the Sky Hawk's daring robbery and their rescue of the air mail flyer were the talk of the town. Before noon, Tim was visited by Hunter, who was not only manager of the local field, but representative for the Transcontinental company.

Hunter looked worried and his words bore out his looks.

"This Sky Hawk is getting to be a nuisance," he told Tim. "He's picked us for $500,000 and although we had it covered by insurance, it doesn't help matters any. Old Tom Blair, who heads our company, has wired me to use every means to apprehend the Sky Hawk. The police and state officials are doing all they can, but the very nature of his operations leaves them almost helpless."

"Flying cops are something for the future," smiled Tim.

"And that's just what we need," went on Hunter. "I want you to agree to help me all you can. Keep your eyes peeled and your ears close to the ground. You may be able to turn up something the police can't uncover. And remember, Tim," he grinned, "there'll be something more than just the fun of a story if you get the Sky Hawk."

"You know I'll do everything I can," replied Tim, as Hunter, weighed down with his worries, said goodbye.

But the Sky Hawk seemed to have dropped from sight. There was a dearth of news and the managing editor cast anxious eyes about for interesting material with which to fill the columns of his paper.

Ever since he had been given the assignment as the flying reporter, Tim had cherished the hope that some day he would be given permission to write a daily column on aviation. That day had been particularly quiet and devoid of stories with interest and to Tim it seemed the right time to approach his managing editor.

After the rush of the final edition had subsided and the presses were roaring their symphony of news, Tim accosted the managing editor.

"I'm sure I can give you a column of live news about aviation every day, Mr. Carson," he said. "We're not running very heavy on news right now and if you'll give me the space, I'd like to show you what I can do."

"When would you have the time to handle it, Tim?" asked the managing editor. "I couldn't spare you for two or three hours every day for that."

"I'm not asking for that," replied Tim. "If you'll give me a column, I'll write the stories after hours and in the evening. I know most of the flyers at the field here and then with the chaps who are flying the air mail, there is an unlimited field for human interest stories. On top of that, I'm keeping right up on all the developments of aviation. All I need is the space, Mr. Carson!"

"When do you want to start it?" asked Carson.

"Any time you can give me the room."

"Can you whip a column of material into shape by tomorrow morning?"

"Easily."

"Then have about three pages of copy ready in the morning." The action was characteristic of Carson. In fact, it was characteristic of newspaper work with its quick decisions and demands that to any class of men but reporters would have been insurmountable.

To Tim the demand for a column of copy in the morning was the best news in weeks and he turned away from the managing editor after expressing his appreciation for the opportunity.

"Oh, Tim," called Carson. "Better stop on your way down stairs and tell the engraving department to work up one and two column heads for you. Have them draw a picture of a plane and put your name under it: By Tim Murphy, the Flying Reporter of the Atkinson News."

Getting together a column of interesting, readable material on such short notice would not be easy, especially since Tim wanted his first column to be alive with interest. After conferring with the head of the engraving department, Tim hurried out to the municipal field where he imparted his good luck into the ever-sympathetic ear of Hunter, the field manager.

"That's fine, Tim," congratulated Hunter. "I know you've wanted to write a daily column on aviation for a long time. Do you think Carson will make it a permanent feature of the paper?"

"That all depends on what kind of material I can dig up and how well I can write it. Means you fellows here at the field will have to cooperate with me."

"You know we'll do that Tim," promised Hunter. "The boys all like you mighty well. The only thing is that they are a bit bashful in telling some of their own experiences. You may have to pry around a bit."

"I expect you're right there," agreed Tim, "but after I get them started I'll get plenty of material. Now I've got to line up a good feature to start the column off tomorrow. You know of anything unusual here at the field?"

Hunter scratched his head and looked meditatively at a cloud as if seeking inspiration.

"Afraid I'm not much help right now," he said. "Say, wait a minute. We'll go over to the radio shack and see if there are any late bulletins on planes coming in tonight."

Tim agreed and they walked over to the little building at the foot of the radio towers where the department of commerce maintained a station, part of its transcontinental link of communication to advise airmen on weather conditions and report the movements of aircraft along the main skyways.

The operator on duty greeted them cordially and turned his file of messages over to them. Hunter thumbed through the flimsy sheets of tissue with experienced fingers. He stopped and read one of the communications with interest. Then he turned to Tim.

"Here's something that came in within the last hour," he said. "May be just what you need for a story."

Tim read the tissue and glowed with excitement at what he read. What a lucky break for him. According to the report, Arthur Winslow, king of the air mail flyers, would land at the local field within two hours for an overnight stop.

"That's just what I need," exclaimed Tim. "Why Winslow is rated as the ace of all airmen. It will make a great yarn if he'll talk."

"There may be some trouble on that point," said Hunter. "I know Winslow only slightly for he's flying on the west end of the transcontinental now, and he's mighty reticent when it comes to talking about himself. It says here that he is ferrying a new passenger and mail plane west."

"Good thing I have a car here," said Tim. "If I can't get a chance at him any other way I can offer him a ride to the city and he can hardly refuse to talk then."

"I think he'll help you out if you explain what you want and how badly you need a good story for the first day your column is printed."

They went into Hunter's office where the manager of the field busied himself at his desk. Tim dug into the files to secure, in advance, all of the available material he could about Arthur Winslow, airman without peer.

The ace of the air mail pilots was not a sensational flyer in the sense that his name was on the front pages of the newspapers every day. In fact, he was just the opposite and as he often told his friends, he didn't care anything about being the best air mail flyer. All he wanted was to be the oldest.

Winslow had trained Col. Charles A. Lindbergh when he was a fledgling and before the flying colonel had even dreamed of a flight to Paris, and he had performed many a heroic deed as he winged his way across the plains of the middle west of the snow-capped Rockies and the rugged Sierras.

Tim was still finding valuable material in the files when a mechanic stuck his head in the door.

"Here comes Winslow," he announced and Tim and Hunter promptly deserted the office and took their places at one side of the big concrete apron which marked the end of the main runway on the field.

The plane rapidly took form as it roared out of the east. Winslow swung low over the field to sight the wind sock, then lined southwest and floated down to a three point landing. There was nothing startling in the way he handled his plane but his every move revealed the hand of a master birdman.

After Winslow had given his orders to the mechanics, he greeted Hunter.

"Winslow," said the field manager as he introduced Tim, "here's a young newspaper man I want you to know, Tim Murphy of the Atkinson News. I think Tim is unique in the newspaper world. He's not only a mighty good reporter but a fine flyer."

Both Tim and Winslow smiled at Hunter's introduction and Tim felt a friendly tingle as he grasped Winslow's hand.

"I've heard of you," said Winslow.

"And I've heard a great deal about you," replied Tim, "so I guess that makes us even."

"Tim's up against a tough proposition," said Hunter as they strolled toward the office. "He wants to run a daily column of aviation in his paper and only today convinced his managing editor that it ought to be given a trial. As a result, Tim has to have a column of material ready early tomorrow morning. On top of that, he's going to do this aviation column on his own time. He wants it to go over big and become a permanent part of the paper and so do I. Down here at the field we think it would be a fine thing and when we saw you were coming in for an over-night stop, we figured you might be able to give Tim some material that would be mighty readable."

"I don't think I've done anything very remarkable or anything that would make good newspaper reading," laughed Winslow, "but if you're willing to have dinner with me up town, Murphy, we'll see what we can dig up."

Tim was pleased at the invitation and accepted it at once. He was having even better luck than he had dared dream, and he felt that given enough time with Winslow, the famous pilot would loosen up and tell him some of the experiences he had had in his eighteen years of flying.

Hunter excused himself, saying that he had work at the field which required his attention, and Tim and Winslow got into the car Tim had brought to the field, and started for town.

They talked of the recent developments in aviation and of the great increase in the number of air mail lines, but it was not until they were at dinner that Winslow really started to unburden himself in answer to Tim's questions.

"When did I start to fly?" mused the veteran of the skyways. "Why that's so long ago I've almost forgotten the date. You young fellows think of flying as a development since the war, but I started flying back in 1912 in the days before we had ailerons on the wing tips and used to warp the wings of our planes to control them."

"You've flown more than anyone else, haven't you?" queried Tim.

"I believe I have," was Winslow's quiet reply. "My record book shows more than 12,000 hours in the air for a little better than 1,400,000 miles. That would be a long time and a long ways if it were a continuous flight," he smiled.

Tim liked Winslow when he smiled. There was nothing of the boaster in this man who was the king of the air. His brown hair looked a little faded from exposure in thousands of hours of sun and wind and storm, and there were decided wrinkles on his face, but his eyes were a clear brown that invited confidence in their owner.

When Tim mentioned the air mail, he struck an especially responsive chord in Winslow's mind, whose life, for the last ten years, had been a part of the mail. He had flown the first mail plane from New York to Washington and later had been one of the pioneer flyers on the transcontinental.

"Those early days were when we got our thrills," reminisced Winslow. "We were flying in cast-off army planes that the post office department had picked up. Our limit was under five hundred pounds of mail and we never had to worry about being overloaded at that. After the old army DeHaviland's were put on the junk heap we got Douglas cruisers and there was a little more regularity to the way we maintained our schedules. When the post office department turned the air mail over to private contractors, we were given the best planes money could buy."

"The air mail's grown immensely popular in the last two years hasn't it?" asked Tim.

"Immensely is hardly the word," said Winslow. "Universally is better, and it's all since Lindbergh flew the Atlantic and focused popular interest on aviation. Why this new plane I'm ferrying west is capable of carrying six passengers and 1,500 pounds of mail and maintaining an average speed of 130 miles an hour. In two years it will be obsolete and we'll have bigger and faster planes in its place."

"Didn't you take a mail plane several years ago and brave a Lake Michigan storm in mid-winter to take food to fishermen marooned on an island?"

"I was lucky," was Winslow's simple reply. "By the way, I've read recently how you did a similar stunt only you dropped supplies to a village cut off by a flood."

"That was luck, too," smiled Tim. "Now I'd like to know if you've ever had any accidents."

"One," admitted Winslow after some deliberation. "It was pretty serious and I don't know whether I ought to give it to you or not. But I guess it won't do any harm," he added and smiled.

"Someone," he said, "parked a plane in the middle of the field at Blanton one night and when my landing lights didn't work I ran into it head-on. Result, two damaged planes and one bad temper."

"You mean that's the only accident you've had in more than a million miles of flying?" asked the incredulous Tim.

"That's all and that's enough," said Winslow. "Flying is safe if you take the proper precautions. The chaps who get cracked-up are stunting, have inferior equipment, or are just plain dumb."

"What," asked Tim, "would be the most thrilling flight to you?"

"A hop over the top of the world," replied Winslow. "I've always wanted to make an Arctic flight and even though Wilkins and Eilson made the trip from Point Barrow to Spitzbergen, I'm not entirely convinced that there isn't land somewhere up there. It would be worth a try, anyway," and his dark eyes glowed with enthusiasm.

Tim felt a peculiar warmth and thrill of inspiration and Winslow's words fell on far more fertile soil than he ever dreamed.

"There's just one more question?" said Tim. "Didn't you help train Lindbergh to fly?"

"Yes, some. We were on the same division of the air mail and saw quite a lot of each other before he flew to Paris."

"What kind of a fellow was he then?"

"Not much more than a kid, quiet and serious minded. If he had any thought of flying to Paris when I knew him, he certainly kept it a secret. He's a wonderful flyer; uses his head and knows every trick in the game."

They had completed their dinner and Winslow, who was obviously tired from a long day in the air, asked Tim if he had all the material he needed for his first column.

"Reams of it, thanks to you," said the flying reporter.

"I'm glad if I have been of any help," replied the veteran of the air mail. "I think the column will be a fine thing. I hope you make a success of it, and I'm sure you will. I'm going to turn in now and get a few hours of sleep."

Tim had been too fascinated with their conversation to take notes during the dinner but it would have been a waste of effort for he could remember clearly every scrap of the information Winslow had given him. He hurried to his room, gathered up half a dozen books Dan Watkins had loaned him to study, and then headed for the copyreader's rooming house.

He found Dan, in dressing gown and carpet slippers, enjoying a novel.

"What's up, Tim," asked Dan.

"Need some advice and also brought your books home," replied Tim. "Carson is going to let me try a daily aviation column to see how it goes. I've got more material than I can possibly use for the first time. Just interviewed Arthur Winslow, dean of the air mail flyers, and have some stuff that will make wonderful copy."

"How much space will you have?"

"Just an even column and I've enough dope for three or four," said Tim enthusiastically.

"That's going to be a job, then," said Dan, "for you must keep within the limits of your space. But that means your story will be even the better—not an extra word or phrase. Here, use my typewriter and get busy."

Tim welcomed the suggestion and for an hour he worked diligently, cutting and rewriting as the copyreader suggested. When he had completed his task he had a column story about Winslow—a column that was fairly alive with the romance of the air mail and of the flyer who was the master of all birdmen.

"Carson will like this, you see if he doesn't," was Dan's comment as he finished reading Tim's work. "Keep this up and it won't be long until you'll be the aviation editor of the News."

"Do you really think so, Dan?"

"I'm sure of it. Only the other day Carson was talking about you and I told him how you were going to night school four evenings every week and that I was suggesting books for you to read. He was well pleased. There aren't many of the boys on the paper who are working like you to get ahead."

Tim reached the office early the next morning and placed his copy on Carson's desk before the managing editor arrived. The directing editorial genius of the News said nothing about Tim's first story but after two or three days he stopped beside the flying reporter's desk one morning.

"The aviation stories you're turning out are good stuff, Tim," he commented. "If you have a little more than a column some days don't hesitate to run over your usual amount of space."

From the fact that Carson was willing to give him more space, Tim knew that his work was finding favor. But he hoped for the day when the managing editor would make it a permanent feature.

Tim worked every extra minute getting material for his column. He interviewed all the famous pilots who landed at the field, wrote sketches of the flyers on the regular air mail runs, and described flights over the city and the surrounding towns. The latter stunt made a great hit with the circulation manager, who personally made a trip to the editorial office to commend Tim. Every town visited and written up from the air meant the sale of more copies of the News.

With his regular work and his studies, Tim found the task of gathering and writing the material for the column a real drain on his physical energies.

"Better take things a little easier," cautioned Dan, but Tim was too much interested in his work and studies to give up anything and he was too conscientious to slight either.

When Tim's health started to suffer under the burden, Dan took the matter in his own hands and went to the managing editor.

"Tim's working too hard," he told Carson. "The boy is too ambitious for his own good and unless you do something he'll work himself to death.

He's doing his usual work in the office, writing his daily column and going to night school four times a week. That's more than he can stand, especially this hot weather."

"I'm glad you called it to my attention," said the managing editor. "I've been very much pleased over Tim's column and it's made a hit with the business office. We decided to make a little change last night and this is a good time to tell Tim about it. Come along."

They walked down the editorial room together until they reached Tim's desk where the flying reporter, his eyes red-rimmed from lack of sleep, was working.

"Hold up a minute, Tim," said the managing editor. "I have some news for you. We're going to discontinue your column."

"But Mr. Carson," protested Tim. Then he stopped abruptly, his tired eyes welling with tears.

"Oh, I'm sorry, Tim, I shouldn't have said it in that way," Carson hurried on. "What I meant to tell you is that the column is gone for good—from now on it will be a regular department of the paper and you're to have charge of it."

CHAPTER NINE

Relieved of the burden of his other duties, Tim devoted all of his energies to the development of his aviation department. He chronicled the arrival and departure of the mail and express planes at the field in addition to all of the private ships which made overnight stops or called for supplies. He also made it a point to use the plane in covering the dedication of every new airport in the state and thus created much good will for his paper.

One day early in May the telegraph editor handed Tim a short story which had just come in over the wire. Its contents were such that Tim picked up the sheet of copy and started for the managing editor's desk.

Carson was closing his desk and preparing to leave the office when Tim accosted him.

"Oh, Mr. Carson," said the flying reporter. "I'd like to talk with you for a few minutes."

The managing editor glanced at the clock. "I haven't much time, right now," he said. "I have an appointment at the dentist's in ten minutes."

"It won't take long," explained Tim and he handed the folded paper to the managing editor, indicating the article which had attracted his attention.

Carson scanned the item and then re-read it, his news sense instantly aroused to the value of the idea behind the story. He smiled at Tim.

"I'll bet you want me to send you and the News' plane on this good will air tour," he said when he had completed reading the story for the second time.

"That's it exactly," enthused Tim. "It seems to me like a great chance. Good publicity for the News and at the same time boosting aviation. According to the tentative plans, this will be a good will air tour of the state, open to every licensed pilot and plane, with stops at all of the larger airports in the state."

"Wouldn't it be pretty expensive?" asked the managing editor.

"Not necessarily," replied Tim. "Gas and oil would be the main item of expense and the advertising value of having a plane in the tour would more than offset the expense."

He's doing his usual work in the office, writing his daily column and going to night school four times a week. That's more than he can stand, especially this hot weather."

"I'm glad you called it to my attention," said the managing editor. "I've been very much pleased over Tim's column and it's made a hit with the business office. We decided to make a little change last night and this is a good time to tell Tim about it. Come along."

They walked down the editorial room together until they reached Tim's desk where the flying reporter, his eyes red-rimmed from lack of sleep, was working.

"Hold up a minute, Tim," said the managing editor. "I have some news for you. We're going to discontinue your column."

"But Mr. Carson," protested Tim. Then he stopped abruptly, his tired eyes welling with tears.

"Oh, I'm sorry, Tim, I shouldn't have said it in that way," Carson hurried on. "What I meant to tell you is that the column is gone for good—from now on it will be a regular department of the paper and you're to have charge of it."

CHAPTER NINE

Relieved of the burden of his other duties, Tim devoted all of his energies to the development of his aviation department. He chronicled the arrival and departure of the mail and express planes at the field in addition to all of the private ships which made overnight stops or called for supplies. He also made it a point to use the plane in covering the dedication of every new airport in the state and thus created much good will for his paper.

One day early in May the telegraph editor handed Tim a short story which had just come in over the wire. Its contents were such that Tim picked up the sheet of copy and started for the managing editor's desk.

Carson was closing his desk and preparing to leave the office when Tim accosted him.

"Oh, Mr. Carson," said the flying reporter. "I'd like to talk with you for a few minutes."

The managing editor glanced at the clock. "I haven't much time, right now," he said. "I have an appointment at the dentist's in ten minutes."

"It won't take long," explained Tim and he handed the folded paper to the managing editor, indicating the article which had attracted his attention.

Carson scanned the item and then re-read it, his news sense instantly aroused to the value of the idea behind the story. He smiled at Tim.

"I'll bet you want me to send you and the News' plane on this good will air tour," he said when he had completed reading the story for the second time.

"That's it exactly," enthused Tim. "It seems to me like a great chance. Good publicity for the News and at the same time boosting aviation. According to the tentative plans, this will be a good will air tour of the state, open to every licensed pilot and plane, with stops at all of the larger airports in the state."

"Wouldn't it be pretty expensive?" asked the managing editor.

"Not necessarily," replied Tim. "Gas and oil would be the main item of expense and the advertising value of having a plane in the tour would more than offset the expense."

"I wouldn't be surprised but that you are right, Tim," said Carson. "I've got to hurry along for that appointment. I'll consider your plan tonight and let you know first thing in the morning."

That evening Tim told Ralph of his hope that the News would enter its plane in the good will air tour and Ralph agreed that it would be a great stunt, both from the standpoint of advertising the paper and of popularizing aviation.

Tim was busy on a handful of rewrites from the morning papers when the managing editor stopped at his desk the next day.

"We've decided to enter our plane in the air tour," he said. "I talked it over with Mr. Adams, the advertising manager, and he agrees that it is an excellent plan. I'm glad you called it to my attention, Tim. We'll work out the details later."

When Tim completed his work on the rewrites he presented himself before the managing editor's desk.

"Sit down, Tim," said Carson, as he indicated a chair at his side.

"We want plenty of local interest in the air tour," he went on, "so what do you think of having a contest to select a name for our plane?"

"That sounds fine, Mr. Carson," replied Tim heartily. "It ought to arouse interest here because Atkinson is getting more and more air-minded. You ought to see the number of people who come out to the field every day to watch the planes, and especially when the transcontinental air mail comes in. There's a fascination about flying that's getting into everyone's blood."

"You certainly have a real case of it," laughed the managing editor, "but I'm glad you have, Tim, for you are doing fine work."

"Now," he continued, "I want you to take complete charge of the contest over the naming of our plane. Offer $100 in prizes to be distributed in any way you see fit. We want to stage the contest in one week and you can have a column a day for your publicity stories. Select your own judges and give me a name by next Thursday. Let's see, this is Tuesday, that will give you two days to get ready, announce the contest this Thursday and the winner in one week. How does that strike you?"

"Dandy, Mr. Carson, and thanks a lot for the opportunity."

Tim threw all his energy into formulating plans for the big contest and by Monday morning, three days before the announcement of the winning name, his desk was piled high with letters. The deadline for entries was set for Wednesday at 6 p. m. with the announcement of the winner in the next day's paper.

The first prize was $50, the second best name would get $25, while the next 25 would be given honorable mention and $1 apiece. Tim selected Carl Hunter, "Tiny" Lewis, the mail pilot, and Ralph to help him open the letters and judge their contents. By the time the final mail arrived Wednesday afternoon more than 5,000 letters had been received and excitement was at a high pitch. A big picture of the plane had appeared in the editions of that day with a question mark on the side where the winning name would be placed.

All evening long Tim and his helpers ripped open letters, scanned their contents, and sorted them as they thought best. It was early morning when they had completed their task and narrowed the 5,000 suggestions down to 27 letters. Out of that 27 would come the first and second place winners and the list of 25 honorable mentions.

Each one of the judges read the 27 letters and then wrote down his choice for the first prize. Tim gathered up the four slips. They were all alike; every one had agreed on the name for the plane, the Good News.

When Tim informed the managing editor of the prize winning name, Carson was elated.

"Great," he bubbled, "great! Couldn't have been better if I had named it myself. That ought to make a real hit."

The managing editor's hunch was right and for the next two or three days there was a steady stream of visitors at the airport to inspect the Good News. The contest and the appropriateness of the name caught the public fancy.

With the success which attended the selection of a name for the plane, Carson gave Tim free rein in writing stories of the good will air tour which was to start from Prairie City, the state capital, and finish at Atkinson. Tim, by dint of much correspondence, persuaded the officials in charge of the tour to bring it to a close at Atkinson instead of going back to Prairie City. The chamber of commerce woke up to the possibilities of the air tour. Tim was frequently consulted and the News occupied a prominent place in the preliminary arrangements.

The day before Tim was to start for Prairie City to join the air tour, Carson called him to his desk.

"Better take Ralph with you," he suggested. "He can relieve you of the burden of writing a lot of the stories and can also help you in piloting. I'll have him take a high speed camera and he may be able to get some good action pictures of planes in the clouds."

Tim welcomed the suggestion that Ralph accompany him for there would be plenty for two reporters to do and the managing editor had indicated that he wanted the tour fully covered. That would mean two or three columns of news a day in addition to about 250 miles in the air with an average of four stops a day for each of the five days on the tour.

When Tim and Ralph reached the airport the next morning ready to start for Prairie City, the state capital and starting point for the good will tour, they found Kurt Blandin waiting for them.

"Hello Murphy," greeted the head of the Ace flying circus. "Little surprised to see me?"

"Why, yes, Blandin," admitted Tim. "You're more or less of a lone wolf and a stranger at this field."

"Right," smiled Blandin and in spite of himself, Tim couldn't help liking the other for the moment. "I'm entering a plane in the tour and since you fellows were going, thought you'd better know my flyer." Blandin called to a slightly built man who had been working over the motor of a nearby biplane.

"I want you to know Daredevil Dugan," said Blandin when the other flyer joined them. Ralph and Tim acknowledged the introduction but Tim felt an instant wave of dislike for Dugan. The air circus flyer who was going on the tour was short of stature, with a peaked face and eyes that shifted constantly. There was no question about Dugan's ability as a flyer for he had a reputation as a daredevil, but there might easily be some question about his ethics.

"I'd like to make the trip," said Blandin, "but I have to ride herd on the bunch of flying lunatics I've got over at my own field. Let them alone and they might decide to make a raid on the treasury."

"I'm not so sure they wouldn't get away with it," added Tim. He was surprised at the effect his words had for Blandin's face clouded with a sudden fury that shook his entire body.

"What do you know about my outfit?" he said hoarsely.

"Nothing," admitted Tim. "But I'd like to know a whole lot more."

With that he turned and walked over to the Good News.

"Why did you stir Blandin up like that?" asked Ralph.

"I honestly don't know," replied Tim. "Maybe it hasn't got me anywhere and maybe it has." He glanced toward the plane Blandin was entering in the air tour and saw the head of the flying circus talking with Dugan. "One thing, though," he added, "I'm going to keep my eyes on Dugan."

When Tim and Ralph landed the Good News at Prairie City, they found thirty-one other flyers and planes registered for the tour. One side of the big field was lined with the heavier-than-air craft. At one end a sport monoplane was almost lost under the wings of a giant tri-motor and there were cabin planes of almost every type represented. The planes were classified in three groups according to the displacement of their motors but that arrangement did not affect the Good News for Tim and Ralph were not competing for the prizes offered to the flyers with the best elapsed time in each class.

They secured a complete list of the flyers and their planes, dug up interesting bits about the famous pilots in the tour, and dispatched their stories to the News that night.

The morning for the start of the state's first air tour was bright and clear, with a soft May wind out of the south; a veteran air man by the name of "Spin" Beeker, gave the pilots their final instructions and then waved them off the field at one minute intervals.

The air was alive with the throbbing of motors, now low, then rising to a crescendo as each pilot tested his plane, then gunned it hard for the takeoff. The Good News was No. 18 in the starting order and Tim sped down the field and into the air on the first lap of the five day tour.

The first night found them at Rollins, a crowded factory town, with 325 miles and three other stops, behind them. The first day had been successful without even a motor failure reported for any one of the 32 planes.

On the second day one plane threw a connecting rod through its crankcase and was forced down in a corn field while on the third day another pilot washed out his landing gear when he came down on the field at Marion.

The noon stop on the fourth day was made at Newton where the flyers were given a reception and dinner in the hangar at the airport. They were late in getting away for the two afternoon hops and Beeker was sending them away at half minute intervals. When he waved his flag at Tim, the flying reporter opened up his throttle and sent the Good News scooting down the field. The sound of another motor, near at hand, drew Tim's attention for a moment.

Some pilot, evidently mistaking Beeker's signal for his own, was speeding down the field for a takeoff. Evidently he had not seen Tim for in another second their courses would converge. Tim, acting by instinct, pulled his stick back hard and at the same time jammed the throttle to the end of its arc.

It was a risky thing to do but he fairly jerked his plane off the ground. The Good News shot skyward, then settled rapidly, but Tim leveled off and after a shaky moment, was heading for the next control point. He had fairly hopped his plane over the other ship. It had been a master bit of flying.

Tim was unable to identify the other plane and it was not until they landed at Beldon, the night stop, that he learned the name of its pilot.

Tim and Ralph had hardly climbed from their plane when "Daredevil" Dugan, accosted them with bitter words.

"Whoever told you two pencil pushers you could fly," he cried. "What do you think this is, a game of Washington tag? You came mighty near wrecking me back there at Newton."

Dugan's attitude angered Tim, who felt that he was in no way responsible for the mixup which had occurred at the noon control station. Before he could answer someone else joined in the party.

"What's this you're saying, Dugan?" The voice was cold with sarcasm and "Daredevil" Dugan swung around to face "Spin" Beeker, the head judge. "Don't you think you'd better pull in your oars," continued Beeker. "I've a good mind to disqualify you for that stunt you pulled back at Newton. Trying to blame these boys, are you? Not while 'Spin' Beeker's judging this tour, you won't."

"You deliberately jumped your flag," he accused Dugan, "and if Tim says you go out, out you go. What do you say, Tim?"

Tim knew that Dugan had a good chance to win first prize in the Class C division for small planes and the call down the field judge had given the "Daredevil" more than satisfied him for the injustice he felt from Dugan's accusation.

"Oh, that's all over now, Mr. Beeker," said Tim. "Only a misunderstanding and it's better to forget all about it."

"Just as you say," agreed the head judge, as he turned back to Dugan, but the Daredevil was already on his way.

Tim watched Dugan as he hurried toward a waiting car. Was it possible that the Daredevil had deliberately attempted to crash them? His thoughts flashed back to the scene at the Atkinson airport and his words with

Blandin. Could the boss of the flying circus have instructed Dugan to get them? It was a question Tim himself couldn't answer and he decided to let things take their course after promising himself that he would keep a closer watch than ever on Dugan.

On the final day of the air tour, Tim, in recognition for his work in promoting the big aviation day at Atkinson, was given the lead-off position and he swept away from the Beldon airport at the head of the caravan of thirty planes.

When familiar scenes again came into view and Tim sighted the field at Atkinson, he was astounded at the size of the crowd which had gathered to see the end of the tour. Every side of the field was jammed with cars, parked row on row, and police and national guardsmen were hard put to keep the milling thousands from sweeping on to the landing field.

Tim had pushed his plane hard and was nearly ten minutes ahead of the others. To keep the interest of the crowd he stunted over the field, looping, falling and zooming in manoeuvres that had the crowd gasping for breath. When he saw the first of the planes in the tour heading in from the west, he nosed down for the field.

Ping! For a second Tim did not realize what had happened. Ralph, in the forward cockpit, had heard the noise and he looked around at the flying reporter. Tim wiggled his stick and it was then that he discovered their predicament. The main control wire to the ailerons on the left wing had parted and was dangling from the wing. By rare good luck the Good News had been in an easy dive when the accident occurred and had leveled off of its own accord.

Below, Tim could see the banked masses of humanity. They'd come out for a thrill, had they? Well, they'd get it but he didn't dare risk a crackup in the crowd. The slogan all through the tour had been to play safe and now here he was up better than 3,000 feet and with a slim chance of getting down alive.

Ralph had sensed what they were up against and was staring back, the color drained from his face. Tim wondered what his own face looked like. Probably he was just as white as Ralph for he was sure enough up against it. What irony! After spending days promoting the aviation day to mark the close of the air tour, then an accident like this. If he could only get his hands on that strand of loose wire he might be able to get the ship down after all.

Tim motioned to Ralph, who leaned back until the flying reporter could make his shouts understood. Ralph's eyes got as big as cart wheels and his mouth dropped open but he nodded and took a firm grip on his nerve.

Carefully the two men in the little plane started to move. Tim thanked his lucky stars that Ralph was a competent flyer and he was ready to bless his managing editor for his foresight in having another reporter trained as an aviator.

To the 25,000 packed around the airport it was something new in the way of thrills. To Tim and Ralph it meant taking their lives on luck and consummate nerve for they had sacrificed their parachutes to make room for their baggage on the five day tour. Tim edged forward and Ralph slid back. In less than a minute they had exchanged places and Ralph was giving the plane an easy rudder to swing it back toward the airport.

Tim stretched his six feet of muscular body over the side of the forward cockpit as Ralph headed for the field. His nerves were remarkably calm; he felt sure he could accomplish the task before him.

Tim swung both legs over the side of the cockpit. Ralph had throttled the motor down as slow as he dared but even then the blast of air from the propeller tore at Tim. The flying reporter anchored his right foot in the step in the fuselage while his right hand was locked in the safety belt which was too short to go around his body as he swung from the side of the ship.

The broken aileron wire dangled tantalizingly from the wing. Tim gauged his distance and thrust an outstretched hand to grasp it. The wire was just beyond his reach!

CHAPTER TEN

The good will planes were swarming in from the west. In another minute there would be a dozen of them circling over the airport and with his own ship able to manoeuvre with only the greatest difficulty, Tim knew that the arrival of the other planes would add more complications to their plight.

The Good News was wavering unsteadily. At any moment it might slide into a spin in spite of all that Ralph could do to keep it on an even keel. Then it would be curtains! But not if Tim could help it. He was determined to reach the dangling wire if it was humanly possible.

The flying reporter started his body swinging. Ralph screamed at him for the Good News was careening from side to side. But Tim kept on, his body swinging out from the side of the plane like a great pendulum, its swings ever lengthening.

Tim clutched at the broken wire; missed by inches. The next time he'd make it. He had to, he told himself, for every second was precious. They couldn't smash up in the crowd below. He swung again, his fingers outstretched in an effort that wrenched every muscle in his body. He touched the dangling wire, but it slipped through his hand. Then a movement of the plane placed it within his reach again and he gripped the wire between his finger-tips. He heard Ralph's triumphant shout as he tightened his grasp on the wire and felt the plane nose downward, but the world was dancing before his eyes. The strain was intense as he hung on like grim death, his left hand holding and controlling the aileron wire, his other hand and foot anchored to the fuselage.

Down they circled, Tim mechanically manipulating the aileron. Truly he was "riding down" from the clouds. He'd read about it being in the war but had hardly believed it possible. Now he was actually accomplishing the feat and getting away with it—maybe. They weren't down yet. Could Ralph turn the trick and make a safe landing? It would require real skill and a keen judgment of distance and speed.

Tim glanced back at his chum and Ralph nodded reassuringly. He knew as well as Tim that if he landed too hard Tim would be bounced off the plane and even an Irishman, and a reporter at that, doesn't like to be thrown from a plane landing at a speed of seventy miles an hour.

Ralph straightened out and headed for the field. Tim steadied himself and uttered a prayer as they dropped closer to the ground. They were over the edge of the field and nosing down fast. Tim glanced at the crowd—a sea of upturned faces. He gave the aileron a final jerk and shut his eyes.

Bang! Crash! Bump! And they were down. The shock of the rough landing threw Tim against the fuselage and he clung there like a plaster. Ralph managed to taxi the Good News across the field and brought it up in front of the announcer's stand and they tumbled down. Above them the sky was alive with planes. They had turned the trick just in time.

Before the crowds surrounded them and swept them toward the announcer's stand, Tim had a second to examine the aileron wire. The break was clean-cut; no frayed ends to indicate an accident due to normal wear and tear. The only thing that could have caused a break like that was a sharp file wielded by spiteful hands.

Tim was so mad he couldn't talk but by the time they found their managing editor, he had cooled down somewhat. They explained what had happened and then Tim swept Ralph off his feet when he told Carson about his discovery of the filed wire.

"I'm not going to accuse anyone right now," said the flying reporter, his eyes pin points of anger, "But when 'Daredevil' Dugan lands he's going to tell me what I want to know or he'll get the worst beating he ever had." And Tim, moved by emotion, looked fully capable of carrying out his threat.

Tim and Ralph were called to the announcer's stand where they were introduced to the crowd and the master of ceremonies briefly related how they had ridden down from the clouds. A great roar of applause swept over the crowd and Tim was genuinely embarrassed at the ovation.

As soon as they could get away, Tim and Ralph slid out of the stand, and lost themselves in the crowd.

"Have you seen Dugan land?" asked Tim.

"He came in about five minutes ago and is well down toward the other end of the field," replied Ralph. "He's slated to do his daredevil stuff right away so we'll have to hurry if we want to catch him."

They made slow progress through the packed mass of humanity and were not more than halfway down the field when the loud speakers blared out an announcement.

"Ladies and gentlemen," boomed the metallic voice, "you will now see 'Daredevil' Dugan, the prince of thrills, in an aerial exhibition which is without peer."

"It'll be an exhibition without peer when I get my hands on Dugan," muttered Tim as he heard the motor of the Daredevil's plane come to life. There was no chance of reaching Dugan before he started so Tim and Ralph crowded their way to front line places.

Dugan's little biplane shot down the field. The tail flipped into the air and the under carriage sailed clear. Then Dugan bounced his ship up and down as he sped alone, never more than five feet above the ground. It was old stuff but mighty dangerous, especially if the motor failed.

The crowd was yelling and milling excitedly as Dugan's plane neared the fence on the far boundary. Tim wondered how long Dugan would wait before he nosed his ship up. Then he caught his breath for the daredevil was living up to his name.

The biplane shot skyward but Dugan had waited a fraction of a second too long. There was the sharp crashing of wood and to the crowd's amazement and horror, Dugan left his landing gear hanging on the fence. But probably no one was more surprised and startled than the daredevil himself.

Alive to the emergency, Tim forgot his personal feelings toward Dugan and with Ralph at his heels pushed his way to the announcer's stand. There he found a group of perplexed and worried officials who were looking on helplessly while Dugan cruised over the field. The crowd recovered its breath, and, mob-like, got all ready for a real thrill when Dugan landed.

Tim cornered Clyde Bennett, the owner of the great tri-motored monoplane which had been on the good will tour. Tim's plan won Bennett's hearty approval and together they explained it to the officials. Several hesitated but "Spin" Beeker acclaimed it the only way to avert tragedy. When he presented that angle of the situation, the other officials immediately gave their consent. They didn't mind giving the crowd its share of thrills, but at the same time they didn't want tragedy to play a major role in the events of the day if it was humanly possible to prevent it.

While Tim and Bennett warmed up the motors of the great transport plane, Ralph went in search of rope. He was back in less than five minutes staggering under his load. They boosted the coils of manilla into the cabin of the big ship and Tim, who had been delegated to handle the controls, was just taking his place when the fiery little managing editor of the News arrived. Carson had gotten wind of what was in the air and was thoroughly aroused. He collared Tim and Ralph.

"You're crazy," he yelled. "I won't let you go on such a foolhardy trip. You'll all get killed and I can't afford to lose two of my best reporters."

"You're crazy yourself if you think we're not going," shouted Tim in reply. "Some one's got to help Dugan down. They say he isn't carrying a parachute. And besides," he suggested, appealing to Carson's nose for news, "it will make a great story for the paper." The managing editor weakened and waved them on. Ralph banged the door of the cabin and Tim fed the fuel into the eager cylinders of the tri-motor. He was mighty glad now that he had taken a course in handling big ships at the flying school.

While they were gaining altitude, Tim scrawled a note, weighed it down with a wrench, and tied it to a stout, light cord. In less than five minutes they were over the daredevil's plane. Ralph pushed open a window in the cabin of the transport and paid out the cord to which the note was attached. A moment of jockeying and the note was in Dugan's hands. The daredevil tore it from the wrench, read it hastily, and then waved his understanding to his rescuers.

The two planes forged westward, gradually gaining more altitude. They wanted plenty of room and the sun at their backs when they started to give the 25,000 spectators on the ground the greatest thrill of the day—a thrill that would surpass anything on the scheduled program. Five miles west of the airport they swung around, their tails to the setting sun.

Dugan's crippled plane was a little ahead and above the tri-motor. The air speed indicator in the big monoplane pointed to 80 miles an hour. Tim took a fresh grip on the controls while Ralph and Bennett made sure that their ropes were ready.

The gap between the two ships gradually closed. Tim was handling the great tri-motor like a veteran.

The daredevil's plane was now just ahead and a few feet above him. Dugan was looking back at the monoplane and handling his own little plane with the skill of a magician. They were almost together; then Dugan's plane was hidden by the great wing of the tri-motor. Tim moved the controls slightly and held his breath. The monoplane rose gently, there was a rasping bump as the daredevil's ship, minus its landing gear, settled on top of the great gray monoplane.

With a shout, Ralph and Bennett swarmed out of the cabin and onto the wings. While Dugan nursed his motor carefully and kept his ship plastered tight against the wing of the tri-motor, the other two lashed the little biplane down. In the cockpit of the big ship Tim was fighting with his controls.

Carefully Tim pushed the big gray bird along while the men on the wing hurried to complete their task. A careless maneuver, and the biplane might be dislodged and brush them into space. After an eternity for Tim, they scrambled into the cabin with news that they had done everything possible to lash the damaged plane.

Again it was up to Tim. Slowly the tri-motor drifted earthward. Perhaps Tim was the only one of the four who fully realized their new danger and he kept his own counsel and nerved himself for the task ahead. But he couldn't help wondering whether the damaged plane was lashed securely. If there was very much slack in the ropes the ship above would bounce when they landed, smash through the great wing and crush them in a trap that would carry them to their deaths at sixty miles an hour, their landing speed.

While the others were laughing over the thrill of the trip, Tim held their lives in his hands. He was tired, dead tired. The good will trip had been fatiguing and the strain of his sensational landing earlier in the afternoon had taken more of his strength than he had realized. But it was too late now to turn the controls over to Bennett. They were at the edge of the field. Tim killed speed with every trick on the list. The roar of the crowd came to his ears as the tri-motor, with "Daredevil" Dugan's plane resting on top, passed overhead.

The ground loomed before Tim's tired eyes as he swung around into the wind for the landing. The shadows of late afternoon were deceptive and his eyes burned from the strain. He felt himself slipping, losing control; then with a mighty effort he came back. The lives of the other three in the plane, as well as his own, depended on his skill. And he couldn't crack up in front of that great crowd! Tim gave the controls a final twist and placed his trust in the guardian angel who looks after flyers. The heavy under-carriage smacked the ground. Tim heard the wing creak and groan in protest at the weight of Dugan's plane. Involuntarily he ducked.

But the wing held and Tim brought the tri-motor to a stop a little past the middle of the field.

When Tim reached the door of the tri-motor he found Dugan waiting for him.

"Quick, Murphy," said the daredevil. "Come around to the other side. I've got something I must tell you."

When they reached the far side of the tri-motor, Dugan burst forth in voluble explanation.

"Blandin ordered me to crack you up on the tour," he explained. "That's why we almost crashed at Newton. When I didn't get you then, I filed the aileron wires on your ship. I've got to get out now, skip the country. I failed to get you and Blandin will break me in two if he ever finds me. Thanks for saving me just now. I'll repay you some day."

Before Tim could answer, Dugan had slipped away and was lost in the crowd which had surged through the police lines and gathered around the tri-motor. Tim and Dugan were to meet again but under circumstances that even Tim hardly would have believed possible.

CHAPTER ELEVEN

With the advent of late spring, aviation became the news of the day.

Flyers were planning trans-Atlantic hops, endurance tests and Arctic exploration. The adventure which held Tim's interest was the Arctic flight which Capt. Rayburn Rutledge, famed explorer, was planning across the top of the world. Not entirely satisfied with the efforts of other aerial explorers, Rutledge still hoped to find a hidden continent under the ice and snow of the Northland.

A great newspaper syndicate had undertaken to finance his trip and Tim's paper had contributed $1,000. Tim read every word of Rutledge's plans with avid interest, and made a thorough study of the conditions in the Arctic. It was just the flight he had dreamed about ever since Arthur Winslow, dean of the air mail flyers, had planted the seed in his mind only a few months before.

On his trip to the west coast, Rutledge stopped in Atkinson and in his interview with the explorer, Tim learned in detail of the plans for the flight over the top of the world. Then Rutledge soared over the Great Smokies on his way to Seattle, his embarkation point for Alaska.

The big news came unexpectedly. Rutledge had been injured in an automobile accident in Seattle; was definitely out of the flight for that year, yet the plane was ready, fully equipped, supplies had been shipped to the far north, and every detail cared for. The time for the adventure was ripe.

Tim read and dreamed and when his managing editor, speaking for the newspaper syndicate, asked him to take over the flight and carry on, Tim's happiness knew no bounds. He felt it was the opportunity of a lifetime and within an hour after his acceptance, word was sent out on the humming press association wires that Tim Murphy and Ralph Parsons, the flying reporters of the Atkinson News, would attempt the daring Arctic adventure.

Another month elapsed before they were ready to leave Atkinson on the start of their long trip. Tim spent his last evening with Dan Watkins in the quiet of his friend's room.

Dan had gone over all the plans with Tim and agreed that they had an excellent chance to succeed in their mission.

"And here's a bit of good news, Tim," he added, just before the flying reporter took his leave, "I have a hunch that if you succeed Carson will make you the aviation editor of the News."

"You really think so, Dan?" Tim's words reflected his hope and eagerness.

"I certainly do," replied the copy reader. "From what I accidentally overheard this afternoon when he was talking with the business manager, things are all set—providing you succeed."

"Then I'll make it across the top of the world or bust up in the attempt," said Tim determinedly.

The farewells the next day were brief for there is little time on a daily paper for leave-taking and Tim and Ralph were glad that it was so. A few sincere good wishes from Dan and their managing editor, and they found themselves on the Overland limited, bound for the coast where they would embark for the voyage along the coast to Alaska.

A week later when their steamer pulled away from the dock, Tim gazed at Seattle's skyline but his thoughts were in the far north as they churned down Puget sound. He was actually bound for the Arctic! Really going to fly across the heart of the great unknown!

His dream had not been a dream after all but he was sensible enough to realize that only by hard work and the whole-hearted cooperation of Ralph had he been able to turn his dream into a reality. Good old steady Ralph. Perhaps he wasn't the speediest sort of a fellow but he was reliable and could always be counted on in coming through in a crisis. And after all that was what counted on such an adventure as they were facing.

The trip up the coast and into the interior of Alaska was uneventful. When they reached Fairbanks they found that their plane had arrived safely and mechanics were already at work assembling it. Days passed like hours as they made their final preparations and it was June before Tim announced that they were ready to make the first hop of their long trip.

On a bright morning in early June they loaded their equipment into the monoplane, waved goodbye to mechanics who had helped so enthusiastically, and headed northward.

Then—fog!

Cold, bone chilling blasts from the Arctic swirled around the high peaks of the Endicott range and forced the trim, gray monoplane plane up and up. Inside the cabin of the little ship Tim and Ralph were eagerly trying to see through the drifting fog banks ahead and below them. The air was bitter cold.

It seemed hours to them since they had skimmed over the field at Fairbanks, flirted the tail of the plane into the air and headed northward across the heart of Alaska for Point Barrow, the northernmost outpost of civilization in that part of North America. For over an hour the weather had been cold but clear—then the dreaded fog. It had forced them higher and higher until they were almost at the ceiling for their heavily loaded plane. For four hours they had plunged blindly ahead, depending solely on their instruments and hoping against hope that they were still on their course.

Tim pored over his charts while Ralph handled the stick. Even a slight deviation from their course would cause them to miss Point Barrow and either go far out over the Arctic Ocean or come down at some lonely spot in the interior of Alaska.

Tim nudged Ralph and pointed to the clock on the instrument board. They had been in the air a little more than five hours. If the fog would only clear they might sight Point Barrow. But the fog refused to lift.

It was useless to go further north and with a bitter face Tim stared down at the drifting banks of gray. A flight across the top of the world—it was the ambition of his life and now, at the very outset, they were apparently doomed to failure through a whim of nature.

Ralph's features were set in equally bitter lines for he knew how much the proposed flight over the top of the world meant to the young explorer. Even in the face of disaster few words passed their lips.

But now months of planning were worthless before the drifting gray clouds. Helplessly, the men in the monoplane cruised around and around, desperately clinging to the hope that the fog would clear. The minutes were speeding, drinking great gulps of precious fuel and their time in the air was nearing an end.

In less than an hour they would be forced to plunge down through the fog to whatever fate the gods of the air had prepared for them. If luck was with them, they might land without cracking up too badly and with the rifles, concentrated food and snowshoes which they had in the plane preparatory to their hop off from Point Barrow, they might be able to reach Barrow or find some trapper's cabin. They might—but the chances were slim and Tim and Ralph now made no attempt to hide their anxiety.

Half an hour more of gas; half an hour more of life. The chill of the Arctic was creeping into their bones; their faces were white with the cold and the little thermometer on the side of the ship registered well below zero. Anything but pleasant weather for a forced landing and probable smashup.

Then Ralph let out a yell. Far to the right there was a rift in the fog and without a moment's hesitation, he headed for it with the motor on full. They shot downward in a long glide, down and through the walls of gray— down and underneath the fog, which was lifting rapidly.

Ahead of them was the rugged coast of North Alaska and Tim managed to get his bearings. They were not more than eight or ten miles west of Point Barrow. With lighter hearts and a motor that was singing sweetly in spite of the sub-zero temperature, they skimmed along the coast. Less than ten minutes later they swooped low over the huddle of buildings that is Point Barrow and out to the pack ice where they landed, turned around, and taxied back toward the village to be greeted by the handful of Eskimos and the crew of the government radio station.

After hasty greetings, Tim and Ralph, still bundled in their heavy clothes, turned their attention to the plane and refused to leave it until they had satisfied themselves that everything thing was O.K.

Early the next day they were back on the ice, working over the monoplane, repacking their equipment and filling the gas and oil tanks, for now that they were ready, they intended to take advantage of the first favorable weather.

Tim was whistling as he worked in the cockpit, making a final inspection, while Ralph busied himself on the motor. Carefully he checked the equipment, the supply of concentrated food, snowshoes, knives, rifles, and a hood and heater for the motor. A forced landing in the heart of the Arctic would not find them unprepared and the stout, specially constructed wooden cockpit would provide them with a real shelter. He was working with a rifle when Ralph climbed in beside him.

"Motor O.K.?" Tim asked.

Ralph nodded and tucked long legs underneath as he sat down. He watched Tim work over the rifle for several minutes before he spoke.

"What's the use of taking all that stuff?" He pointed to the rifle, the pile of soft-nosed bullets beside it, the snowshoes, the axe and other equipment fastened to the walls of the cockpit. "If we come down out there," and he pointed toward the bleak stretches of the Arctic, "it's curtains for us."

Ralph wasn't trying to hang crepe. He was simply stating the situation as he saw it, tinged with an airman's sense of fatality.

Tim kept on with his work; he knew Ralph well. When he did answer, it was with carefully chosen words.

"Simply this, Ralph, if we come down out there we've still got a good chance of coming through. With snowshoes, this concentrated food, plenty of warm clothing, plus a good rifle and lots of ammunition, we can live for months. Not scared, are you?" The last words were whipped out.

"Scared? Me?" Ralph's question was one of amazement. "I'm not scared and you know it but a 2,200 mile flight over the jumping off place isn't the nicest thing in the world. But I'm here and I'm going through with it."

Tim, laughing at his friend's evident indignation, turned to him. "I know you are, Ralph, and we'll come out on top in the end. Now get out of here and let me stow this stuff away. If the weather is favorable, we'll hop off as soon as we can get some sleep."

Twelve hours later every inhabitant of Point Barrow was down on the ice pack watching the flyers' final preparations. A final inspection, a roar of the motor, and Ralph flirted the tail of the plane around. The motor, on full, drove a cloud of snow and ice into the faces of the little cluster of Eskimos and radio operators, and the monoplane bumped over the ice. It gained speed slowly.

Inside the little cabin Tim and Ralph were straining forward, fairly throwing their energy into the roar of the motor and praying that they would gain air speed.

The skis on the under carriage finally left the rough ice; wobbled in the air for a moment, looking as though they were on the feet of a drunken man, and then plunked to the ice. The plane careened and Tim and Ralph were hurled against the sides of the cabin with sickening thuds as a ski crumpled under the shock and one wing drooped low, almost scraping the ice. Ralph his hands clinging to the controls, was fighting the plane in an attempt to check its speed before any damage could be done.

He finally nosed it up an easy incline of snow and the flyers hopped out to inspect the damage. A minute later they were surrounded by their Eskimo friends. One of the metal skis was damaged beyond repair, and Tim thanked heaven he had had the foresight to put an extra pair in the plane before they left Fairbanks. With the Eskimos to keep the wing on the damaged side from dragging, Ralph got his ship turned around and back at the edge of the ice pack. Their first attempt had failed.

Working feverishly in an effort to replace the damaged ski and to take advantage of the good weather, Tim and Ralph labored on the plane, the numbing cold forcing them to stop at short intervals to warm their chilled hands.

Four hours later they were ready for the second attempt. With the Eskimos cheering as loudly as before, they started over the uneven ice pack. The plane bumped and swayed as it gained speed, calling for all the mastery in the capable hands of Ralph, but it was going faster than on the first attempt. It looked like a sure thing this time, and both young adventurers were congratulating themselves when one ski struck a hummock, the rapidly moving ship swung off its course and before Ralph could right it, dove over a snow bank and headed at right angles to its intended course. By quick work they cut the motor and stopped the plane before it had rammed its nose into a snowbank.

Tim grinned a little ruefully as he looked at Ralph. Two attempts had failed and just when conditions were ideal for their success.

"I'll get this ship off the ice or bust in the attempt!" Ralph had sensed the question in his friend's mind.

The plane had not been damaged and with the help of the willing Eskimos, they pulled it out of the soft snow. It was evident to both Tim and Ralph that it would be impossible to make a take off from the rough ice pack near Point Barrow. Further out on the pack, the ice was smoother and three miles from the village they found a suitable stretch.

Another day was spent in dragging the plane over the ice and clearing away the rough spots on their new field. But when they had finished, they had a smooth runway more than half a mile in length and wide enough for a good margin of safety. A smashup now would mean failure for the year since a new plane could not be secured in time for another attempt.

Tim and Ralph planned to snatch a few hours sleep and then take off, for day and night were one in the Arctic summer.

They had hardly dropped asleep when an operator from the radio station awakened them with the news that a severe storm was reported sweeping down the coast. The adventurers hastily donned their clothes and hurried across the pack where they covered the plane with heavy tarpaulins and staked them down. Tim was loath to desert his ship, but the song of the chill blasts that were sweeping over the ice warned them that it would mean sure death to remain on the windswept pack. After reassuring themselves that they had done everything possible to protect the plane, they started back for Point Barrow on a run.

The cry of the storm was louder, and far in the west the sky was gray with sweeping snow clouds. The flyers struggled on; Point Barrow was less than half a mile away. Then dense curtains of snow swirled about them and Point Barrow might have been a million miles away. The cold was intense; the snow blinding, but arm in arm they staggered on, trying to keep at right angles to the blasts. Ralph was rapidly becoming numb for he had donned only comparatively light clothes when they had started their dash to the plane. Now his feet were dragging and his body chilled to the bone. He was half dazed, too, with the desperateness of their situation. With the village perhaps only a few feet away, the wall of snow shut them in as effectively as though they were in another world. Ralph's feet refused to move and he dropped to the ice, exhausted.

Tim slapped his companion's face, beat his arms and legs, but the aviator's mind refused to respond and he lay helpless. Struggling with his friend, Tim finally managed to swing his body over his shoulders and he staggered slowly on through the swirling snow. His double burden was sapping his strength and his feet were like lead. The end was near. He could hardly put one foot ahead of another.

"One-two, one-two, one-two." Slowly his feet obeyed the command, then refused, and he pitched forward, pinned to the ice by Ralph's body.

They might have been centuries on the ice for all Tim and Ralph knew, but when they came to, they were in the radio station, clothing off and their bodies undergoing snow massages. Neither one had suffered much from the effects of the experience although the Eskimos had found them just in time. Nervous exhaustion more than anything else had been responsible for their collapse on the ice.

The wind and snow raged for three days, and during that time Tim and Ralph spent their hours in sleep and stowing away plenty of good food, for the experience in the storm had warned them that they must have their bodies as well as their minds on edge if they hoped to succeed on their flight over the top of the world.

By the fourth day the skies had cleared, although the cold was intense. As soon as they could get into their clothes, Tim and Ralph headed a party across the ice, anxious to discover what damage the storm might have done to the plane. The tarpaulin-covered ship looked like a model T snow house but when they had removed the snow and the heavy canvas covering, they found the plane intact. The strong wind had swept snow clear of their runway and after warming up the motor and giving it a final test, they were ready for another attempt.

Eskimos were dispatched to the village to bring compasses and extra clothing while Tim and Ralph satisfied themselves that the plane was in perfect condition. When the party from Point Barrow returned, they brought two messages from the radio station. One was that weather conditions were as near perfect as possible and that the storm which had raged for three days had passed down into the Hudson Bay country.

The other message was from their managing editor.

"Eyes of the entire world on your daring attempt. Our every wish for your success.—Carson."

The message cheered both flyers for they well knew the dangers they were about to face.

Tim installed the compasses, unrolled his charts and checked them again while Ralph idled the motor and then ran it up and down the scale with never a miss.

They were ready. The Eskimos jerked the chocks out from under the skis, and the trim little monoplane shot down the smooth runway, bound on one of the most daring flights in the history of aviation!

CHAPTER TWELVE

The plane skimmed over the ice for nearly half a mile, then shot upward in a joyous goodbye to the little group on the ice.

Tim and Ralph smiled at each other. At last they were off the ice, in the air, and started on the 2,200 mile flight over the roof of the world—a flight that was to carry them across the heart of the Arctic, across areas never before seen by the eyes of man. Just what the hours ahead of them held in store they could only guess. Tim hoped that the trip would reveal the age-old secret of the Arctic, whether a hidden continent existed in the land of ice and snow. Ralph hoped that the plane would carry them through to King's Bay, Spitzbergen, their destination.

The pilot kept the stick back until they reached 6,000 feet and then leveled off on their course. The motor was running smoothly, even though the thermometer outside the cockpit windows registered 40 degrees below zero. Underneath them, their shadow was flitting over the rough, broken ice pack at 110 miles an hour. For two hours they roared steadily onward, with only an occasional word, Ralph handling the stick and Tim carefully checking their course, for a variation of one degree would make them miss Spitzbergen, scarcely more than a tiny dot of an island on the other end of their long course.

They were far out on the Arctic ice pack and Tim kept a careful check of his charts while he scanned the rolling sea of ice beneath them for traces of the fabled Arctic continent. At 6,000 feet they had a visibility of 200 miles and he secured some marvelous pictures. For another two hours they forged steadily ahead, conversation at a minimum, although Ralph chewed enthusiastically on a cud of gum.

Tim estimated that they were nearly 500 miles from Point Barrow when they sighted storm clouds far ahead. Great, rolling banks of clouds were piling up over the horizon as the speedy little plane roared on its eastward flight. The air was growing colder and Ralph revved the motor up in an attempt to climb above the approaching storm, but fast though the sleek, gray monoplane climbed, the clouds climbed faster, and, finally, with a shrug of his shoulders that meant more than words, Ralph glanced at his chart and compasses and headed into the storm. Snow and wind buffeted them and the compasses swung wildly as the plane gyrated in the air. For half an hour Ralph fought the controls, a half hour that was centuries long to Tim, who had staked everything on the success of their flight. The clouds thinned and they shot out again into clear weather. The storm had swung them nearly 50 miles further south than they had intended, and Ralph turned the plane northward again. Although they were cutting across the heart of the Arctic, they would not pass over the North Pole, since the only purpose of the flight was to discover whether there was hitherto unknown land in the Arctic.

For hours they droned onward, both young adventurers busy at their tasks. Mile after mile of ice, some of it smooth as glass, other stretches rough and hummocked and sometimes shot with long streaks of open water, unfolded under their eyes. They were flying very high, up nearly 10,000 feet, and the visibility was unusually good. But still there was no land. Only ice and water and more ice. Tim snapped magnificent panoramas of ice and snow that would thrill thousands of newspaper readers if they succeeded.

The cold was bitter but with the motor functioning perfectly neither Tim nor Ralph noticed it. Once in a while they shifted positions to rest their tensed bodies and their conversation was in shouted monosyllables.

Suddenly Tim's elbow went into Ralph's ribs and one heavily gloved hand pointed to the hazy outlines of land far to their right. Ralph nodded and grinned.

"That's Grant land," shouted Tim. "Means we've passed over the heart of the Arctic without finding land. The big job's done. Now all we've got to do is keep on until we reach Spitzbergen."

They had flown over the top of the world and definitely proved that the fabled Arctic continent was just that—a fable.

The northern end of Grant land rapidly assumed definite proportions while Tim completed his log of their flight over the heart of the Arctic.

There was more open water below them now and the lines on Ralph's face deepened, for a forced landing would mean sure disaster. Grant land slipped away beneath them as they pushed steadily eastward while far to the south the mountains of Greenland were rearing their white-crested heads.

Tim went back in the cabin to check up on their gasoline supply, for they were still nearly 600 miles from Spitzbergen. He had just completed testing the tanks when a shout from Ralph made him hurry back to the pilot. There was no need for words. Far ahead, probably 300 miles away, another storm was brewing.

Tim debated only a moment before he turned to his pilot.

"It's up to you, Ralph," he yelled in his companion's ear. "We can buck the storm or turn back and land at Grant land. Plenty of game there to keep us alive and if we can't get the plane off the ice again, we can walk to the station of the Northwest Mounted Police at Bache peninsula."

"I'm not going to do any walking in this temperature," shouted Ralph. "It's Spitzbergen or curtains for me," and he turned back to his controls.

The next two hours were an agony of suspense for Tim and Ralph. Ahead of them the storm clouds loomed higher and higher and half an hour before they reached the storm area, the wind was teasing their plane. But there was no turning around now; only straight ahead for their gas was too low to risk a flight back to Grant land.

Into the heart of the storm they flew; both white faced and tense as they faced the final ordeal of their great flight. The gale tossed their plane through the clouds and driving snow beat on the wings and against the windows of the cabin. Both men were watching the clock on the instrument board, with Tim making anxious trips to the gas tanks. Their fuel supply was running dangerously low.

If only the storm would abate so they could get their bearings. The same prayer was in the minds of both and whether it was an answer or flyer's luck, the clouds lightened a few minutes later and during a lull in the storm, Ralph sent the plane rocketing downward.

At the 1,000 foot level he checked their descent and through the now thinly drifting snow they could discern a savage, broken line of cliffs rearing their heads above the ice pack. Further back were the outlines of a mountain range.

Spitzbergen. Tim let out a shout of relief and Ralph gave the motor the gun in an attempt to find a suitable landing place before the storm closed down again. They shot low over the coast line, but the clouds cut down their visibility and it was impossible to see more than a mile in any direction. Ahead of them the mountains disappeared in the clouds.

Ralph circled desperately, motor thrumming wildly. Finally he found a small, level snow field, well down in an ice valley. It was risky but with the storm and the gas supply nearly exhausted, a landing was the only thing. The pilot banked swiftly, cut his motor, straightened out and then drifted down on the narrow field. The skis touched the frozen snow, bounced once, twice, and then carried them smoothly forward. The plane stopped under one wing of the little valley, well protected from the storm, which was closing down again.

Half paralyzed with cold and fatigue, Tim and Ralph forced themselves out of the plane. Hastily, they examined the ship, then dove into the cabin for an axe, light steel stakes and ropes. In a short time they had the plane staked down securely and had slipped the heavy canvas cover of the heater over the motor. A portion of their precious fuel went to fill the tank of the heater for if the oil in the motor froze their chances of getting into the air again would vanish.

Back in the cabin of the plane they warmed themselves over their alcohol stoves while outside the wind and snow raged at the man-made craft which had slipped through their fingers. Tim opened their supply kit and they munched chocolate and biscuits and topped it off with malted milks made from melted ice. There had been little conversation, but now that the strain of the long flight was over and they were on land again, their lips were unsealed and they discussed the trips and their prospects at some length.

"Storm sounds like a regular old norther and that may mean a week," was one of Ralph's laconic contributions.

"I'm not worrying as much about the storm as I am about our gas supply," said Tim. "We've got enough concentrated food for a couple of weeks but we may not have enough gas to get us any place when it does let up."

"I'm too tired to worry about where we are, gas, food or anything else," and with that Ralph snuggled down in his flying clothes and was soon asleep. Tim adjusted the little stoves, made sure that there was proper ventilation in the cabin, and was in a sleep of exhaustion in a few minutes.

How long they slept neither one knew for when they awoke the clock on the instrument board had stopped, but the storm continued in full strength. The temperature was flirting with the 30 degree below zero mark but in the enclosed cabin they were comfortable. Despite the intense cold and the angry shrieks of the gale, Ralph insisted on dodging out to give the plane a "once over." With an inward feeling of unrest, Tim watched his companion disappear in the storm.

Seconds were minutes and minutes were hours while Tim waited for Ralph to return. He was on the verge of despair when his chum stumbled through the swirling snow and pitched headlong onto the floor of the plane. Ralph was shouting and laughing idiotically. Something in his mind had snapped under the terrific strain of the flight and the pounding of the storm.

Although Ralph continued to shout and once in a while screamed in terror, Tim realized that he was not dangerous and that the trouble was probably a nervous one. He fixed a cup of hot chocolate and the steaming liquid calmed Ralph. Words and phrases became coherent and Tim was astounded by the story he pieced together from his friend's rambling account.

He couldn't doubt Ralph's story—there must be something behind his incoherent narrative—something in the tale of terror that had driven him half mad. But Tim felt that the big thing was to get Ralph calm, to give his nervous system a chance to get back to normal.

For endless hours he sat with Ralph, soothing him as some shriek of the gale alarmed him. In spite of himself, Tim half expected some unknown terror to stalk out of the storm. Could he, too, be losing his senses? He pinched himself and tried to reason that everything was all right but back of all the common sense he could call upon was the fact that Ralph had encountered something far beyond the ordinary. Whatever it was, Tim intended to find out as soon as the storm let up.

Ralph finally sank into a deep sleep of nervous exhaustion and a short time later the storm abated. The wind died down rapidly and the snow ceased its stinging tattoo against the plane. In the gray light Tim could see the dim outlines of the ice walls of the valley which had shielded them from the full fury of the elements.

With Ralph asleep it was his chance to do a little exploring, and, making sure that he was ready for action, Tim slipped out of the cabin. He knew that whatever had terrorized Ralph must be close for the flyer couldn't have wandered far in the storm and found his way back.

Tim skirted the right side of the valley and was halfway back on the left side when he came upon a good-sized opening in the ice wall of the valley. For a moment he hesitated. Without doubt it was something behind the black opening which had so upset Ralph. Determined to solve the mystery, Tim looked at his rifle again, then started resolutely forward. Half a dozen paces inside the mouth of the cave he halted. There was no sound of life— nothing to indicate that some Arctic animal might be waiting to pounce upon him.

Ahead Tim thought the darkness of the cave seemed lighter and he pushed cautiously on, testing every foot of the way for fear he might step in some fissure in the ice. The cave was growing lighter. He turned a corner and stopped involuntarily.

In spite of himself Tim exclaimed aloud at the horror and beauty of the scene that was unfolded before his eyes. Vikings—great giants of men— peered down at him from the prow of their galley, spears in hand, ready to impale him if he moved.

For a minute Tim was motionless. Then he realized that somehow, in centuries long gone, a Viking ship and crew had been caught by the relentless north and entombed by the ice. There they had been for centuries and there they might remain keeping their ceaseless vigil, until the end of time, unless Tim carried the news of his discovery back with him.

No wonder Ralph had been terrorized when he stumbled into the ice tomb. Light that filtered through crevices in the roof gave a weird, unnatural effect that would have shocked the nerves of even the steadiest man. And Ralph had already been under a terrific strain.

Tim stood reverently before the tomb of the men of old. It was evidently the forward watch looking down at him for the prow of the vessel was all that was in view. The rest of the strange craft faded into the shadows of the ice wall of the cave.

The men were physical giants—their crude leather jackets still buttoned close around them to keep out the Arctic cold. Yellow hair peeped from beneath helmets that fitted close to their heads. Long spears were clutched in readiness for a foe that never came and eyes stared over Tim and into eternity.

Tim spent an hour studying his discovery and mentally cataloging all the details. What stories he would have when they got back to civilization. In addition to proving that there was no continent in the Arctic, they had found a tomb of the Vikings.

He hastily ran back for his camera and exhausted the remainder of his supply of plates taking time exposures in the tomb of the north.

Tim knew that if they could safely complete their flight, they would have some of the greatest news pictures in years.

When he finally returned to the plane he resolved to say nothing about his discovery to Ralph when his chum awoke, rested and with his nerves back to normal, Tim was happy to see that his pilot recalled the whole incident as a bad dream. Later he would tell him all about it.

While Ralph took off the hood of the heater and inspected the motor, Tim busied himself working out their location.

"Not as bad as it might be, Ralph," he called. "I've got it doped out we're on an island just off the west coast of Spitzbergen. King's bay is about 100 miles, air line, and we've got enough gas to make it."

"Plenty of gas, if we ever get off this excuse for a landing field," grunted Ralph. He scrambled into the cabin, threw the switches, and Tim swung the propeller. Again and again he leaned on the shiny stick and finally the motor caught with a sputter, then a roar that shrouded the plane in a cloud of snow.

Tim hastily chopped away the lashings and helped Ralph swing the plane around so it headed toward the coast. Down the center of the valley the wind had swept the snow clean and hard, ideal for a takeoff if there was room enough to get the plane into the air before it crashed into the ice on the shore.

Ralph gave the motor a final test and motioned for Tim to climb in. The song of the motor deepened, reached a crescendo, and they started slowly ahead, gathering speed rapidly, and, just when it seemed that they would catapult into the ice, they shot into the air. It was an old trick and Ralph had worked it to perfection.

With the motor working perfectly despite their enforced stay in the valley, they headed eastward and in little more than an hour were skimming over King's Bay.

When they landed, both adventurers tumbled from their plane and raced for the radio station where they made arrangements with the operator to send their stories to the News as fast as they could be written.

Ralph wrote the story of their flight over the top of the world and failure to discover land while Tim wove his discovery of the Viking tomb into a powerful, dramatic tale that within a few hours was to fascinate the reading public of America.

The operator was still busy sending their copy over the ether waves when he stopped for a moment.

"There's a couple of messages for you," he said to Tim. "Shall I take them?"

"Go ahead," replied the flying reporter.

The operator's fingers flew as he copied the messages and then handed them to Tim.

The flying reporter's eyes dimmed and his hands shook as he read the first message, then re-read it to be sure that he was not mistaken.

"To Tim Murphy,
Aviation Editor,
Atkinson News,
King's Bay, Spitzbergen.

Heartiest congratulations on wonderful flight and stories. Effective today you are aviation editor of News with Ralph as your assistant.

(Signed)
George Carson,
Managing Editor."

Tim's heart leaped with joy. Aviation editor of the News! The attainment of his cherished goal.

With trembling fingers he took up the second sheet of flimsy. The words danced before his eyes; they were almost like a message from another world.

"Congratulations. Your flight was splendid. Am awaiting your return. No fun sky-larking when you aren't around to make things interesting. The score is still 50-50. The next time we meet will be the last for one of us.

THE SKY HAWK."

CHAPTER THIRTEEN

Tim kept the contents of the Sky Hawk's message to himself. There was no need to alarm Ralph for he felt that it was a personal matter, but it disturbed him more than he cared to acknowledge. On the verge of what should have been his greatest success, the attainment of the goal to which he had been striving, the aviation editorship of the News, had come the mysterious message from the Sky Hawk, and Tim promised himself that he would keep himself fully prepared and alive to every emergency.

Their return to Atkinson brought a round of banquets and series of speeches at civic clubs. By early fall he was back in the pleasant routine, but this time with a desk of his own and the sign, "Aviation Editor," on a small card.

For days he watched the news, listened to the gossip at the airport but there was no sign of the Sky Hawk—no sign since the day he had looted the wreck of the mail months before in the fastnesses of the Great Smokies. Yet Tim felt that the Sky Hawk was about to strike again and he knew that the next time it would be a battle to the end.

Then the smouldering fires of revolt burst into flame in Mexico. General Enrique Lopez, an officer in the federal army, had broken with the government and had taken the field against the federals. His army, recruited from the ranks of disgruntled federal soldiers, Yaqui Indians and peasants, enjoyed startling success in the first days of the revolution. Then Lopez played his hidden card and bombed Mexico City from the air.

The daring of his feat fanned American interest in the revolt and the front pages of the papers blazed with headlines which told of the progress of the revolt.

Young airmen, attracted by the high salaries offered by both the federal and rebel armies, flocked toward the border, only to be met by the stern, hard flying men of the U.S. army's border patrol. There they were warned to turn back or take their chances at being shot down in their attempt to fly into Mexico. The majority of them returned but a few of the more daring ran the gauntlet of fire from the border patrol and made their way into Mexico.

A few pictures of the fighting between the troops came straggling up from the border but they were far from satisfactory and so far as could be ascertained, there were no actual photographs of the rebel chieftain. Within a short time American news picture services were offering fabulous prices for pictures of General Lopez but the wily rebel leader evaded every effort of the photographers. The luckless individuals who penetrated through his lines were imprisoned and their plates and cameras smashed.

Tim, who had been watching the course of events below the border, was not greatly surprised when, one morning late in August, Carson called him to his desk.

"Can you be ready to start for Mexico in half an hour?" asked the managing editor.

Tim had halfway expected to be sent to the border but to be asked to get into the interior of the strife-torn country was another thing. But his answer was quick in coming.

"In less than that, if it's necessary," he said.

"I'm not ordering you to go, Tim," went on the managing editor. "It's up to you, but it's a great chance for the News to scoop the world if you can get inside Lopez' lines, gain his confidence, and get back here with exclusive pictures of the rebel camp. It will be dangerous and your life will be in your own hands."

"I'll be ready to start in half an hour," was Tim's even-toned reply. Inwardly he was seething with excitement for it was his biggest assignment.

"I was fairly sure you would go," smiled Carson, "but I don't want you to take an unnecessary risk. I've had your equipment ordered, a high speed camera, and plenty of plates for the long distance shots. In addition, we have a small pocket camera that may come in handy if they seize your big machine. Here's plenty of money for expenses on the first part of the trip and we'll authorize the bank at Nogales, Arizona, to honor your checks for any amounts that you may need."

Tim had turned away from the managing editor's desk to tell Dan Watkins of his big assignment when Carson called him back.

"I think you ought to know," he said, "that if you get those pictures we can sell the national rights on them to a news picture service. That will mean several thousand dollars and I'll see that you get a fair share if you succeed."

Dan, at the copy desk, was enthusiastic, but he cautioned Tim to be careful.

"We'll miss you, Tim, and will be looking for your return," he added as they said goodbye.

Tim hurried to his room, gathered the few essentials he would need for the trip, and drove out to the field. There he inspected the cameras and made sure that everything was in readiness for the long flight. It would be a good 1,000 miles to Nogales, on the border, and another 200 miles down into the mountains of Sonora before Tim could hope to come in contact with the rebel forces.

Confident that he had all the equipment necessary for his hazardous undertaking, Tim swung into the cockpit of the Good News. The motor was purring impatiently, as though the plane sensed its mission and was anxious to be clear of the ties that kept it earth-bound.

There were hasty last-minute farewells and then Tim sent his plane dusting over the field and into the air. He was away on his biggest assignment—that of securing pictures of the leader of the Mexican revolt.

The trip to Nogales was uneventful and Tim took two days to cover the 1,000 miles, landing at the border city shortly before noon on the second day. He circled over the airport while one of the ships of the U. S. army border patrol took off and climbed to have a look at him.

When the pilot of the army craft saw the sign on Tim's plane, he waved a friendly greeting and sped away into the east on his lonely patrol.

Tim soared down out of the cloudless sky and brought the Good News to a stop on the brown, sunbaked field at the edge of the city. He went through the usual formality of registering his plane and his credentials were accepted without question.

Before he left the field to run into the city for lunch, an incoming plane attracted his attention. It was one of the border patrolmen, flying fast and low. The machine made a dizzy sideslip and broke one wheel in landing but the pilot managed to check its wild course and brought it to a halt before it crashed into one of the hangars near the main office.

Tim was one of the first to reach the plane and helped pull a white-faced flyer from the cockpit. The army man had been shot through the right shoulder and his arm hung limp and useless. He had managed, somehow, to land with only one hand on the controls.

"What happened, Kennard," demanded Captain John Talbot, commandant of the Nogales field.

"Ran into a chap trying to cross the border," replied Lieutenant Ned Kennard, "and he decided to shoot it out with me. You'll find what's left of him about twenty-five miles west of here."

Tim pieced the story together and secured enough material for a dandy yarn on the first airplane battle along the border. He hastened into town to the telegraph office where he filed a 1,000 word story to the News. When he returned to the field after lunch he found a message from Carson, congratulating him on the story. Tim's yarn had been much more complete than the story carried on the press association wires and had reached Carson's desk two hours before it came through the regular channels. It had enabled the News to score a clean beat on their rival afternoon papers in Atkinson on the big story of the day.

Tim was forced to wait a few minutes before he could obtain an interview with the commandant of the field. When he finally entered Captain Talbot's office, he received a cordial greeting.

"I understand you want permission to cross the border and hope to get pictures of Lopez and his rebel camp," said the commandant.

"That's right," said Tim, "and I'll appreciate all the advice and help you can give me."

"Then my advice is don't go," replied Captain Talbot. "General Lopez is a thoroughly capable military man but his chances of success are slim. Even now he has been driven into the mountains of Sonora and only his air force of a dozen planes has saved him. He may have to make a break for the international border almost any day and he doesn't want his picture broadcast. As it is now, I haven't any idea what he looks like for we have no photographs. But if you succeed in your mission he will be recognized instantly at any border post."

"Do you think the revolution Lopez has started is justified?" asked Tim.

"No, I don't," said Captain Talbot, emphasizing every word. "I've been on the border for ten years now and I know Lopez is nothing more than a bandit, and not a very high class one at that. He's using the revolution as a guise to rob banks, loot towns and generally blackmail all of the business interests in the territory which he controls. It's simply banditry on a wholesale scale and when he gets his pockets filled, he'll slide across the border and leave his subordinates to face the federal firing squads."

"Nice sort of a fellow, isn't he?"

"Yes," said the military man. "Nice when you have him in front of you where you can watch him every minute."

"I've been assigned to get pictures of Lopez and that's what I'm going to do," said Tim. "It looks like I may be helping a lot of poor fellows if I do get those pictures and spread Lopez' likeness all over the front pages."

"I don't envy you the task. You're putting your head in the lion's mouth and you'll be so far down in Sonora that we won't be able to help you. If you were only ten or twelve miles across the border, we might help for we stretch the boundary once in a while when our people get in trouble," said Captain Talbot while a slight smile played around the corners of his mouth.

"I might as well make plans to start first thing in the morning," said Tim, "and if you'll lend me a bucket of dope, I'll paint out the sign on the side of my plane. It would be fatal to go barging into Mexico with that kind of an identification for everyone to shoot at."

Captain Talbot agreed to let Tim have all the material he needed and also assigned a mechanic to help him. By late afternoon the Good News had been completely disguised and some fake bullet holes, to indicate a clash with the border patrol, were made in the wings and the fuselage.

Tim had decided on the role he would play. He intended to stake the success or failure of his plan on a bold approach of Lopez' camp, where he would present himself as a free lance flyer ready to join the rebel cause.

The next morning Tim secured the latest information on the whereabouts of the rebel chieftain and found that Lopez was near Cedros, three hundred miles south of the border and well into the mountains of Sonora. From that guarded retreat he was directing his army while his flyers made raids on the federal troops who were massing for an attack on his mountain stronghold.

With the good wishes of the border patrolmen ringing in his ears, Tim took off from the field at Nogales and headed south, following the line of the Southern Pacific of Mexico. For a hundred miles he followed this course, then angled southeast. In a little more than two hours and a half he was well into the mountains, and according to his map, should be nearing Cedros, the village where Lopez had established his headquarters.

A sharp droning caught Tim's attention and he turned to find a black monoplane bearing down on him. Twin machine guns, mounted on the cowling, were belching tracer bullets in his direction. One thing sure, Lopez' watchdogs of the clouds were on the alert.

Tim had no intention of being shot down and although he was confident the Good News could outrun and out-maneuver the other plane, he concluded he might just as well start his little game. He gripped the stick between his knees and held his hands above his head as the other plane overhauled him.

The pilot of the black craft stopped his chattering guns and motioned for Tim to precede him through a gap in the mountains. In less than five minutes they were over the sheltered valley where the village of Cedros nestled close to the mountain-side. It was an ideal retreat for the rebel chieftain, practically inaccessible to the federal troops and easily defended from the air.

Tim, obeying orders from the other pilot, landed in a small field a short distance from the village. He shut off his motor and waited for his captor to approach. The pilot of the black monoplane was a chunky little man with fiery red hair and watery blue eyes.

"What are you doing down here?" he demanded, as he came up to Tim's plane. He carried a revolver strapped to his waist but made no motion toward it. "You're nothing but a youngster," he added.

"I'm looking for General Lopez," said Tim. "I heard he was paying good money for flyers."

"You've found Lopez all right," said the other airman. "This is his headquarters and unless I'm mistaken, he's hot-footing it down here right now. You'd better tell a straight story or he'll make you wish you were never born."

Tim saw a pudgy, brown-skinned little man in a khaki uniform with an abundance of gold braid, strutting down the road that bordered the field. Trailing him were half a dozen officers of nondescript rank.

"Better climb down," muttered Tim's captor.

The flying reporter slid out of his plane and lounged against the fuselage, as he watched the approach of the rebel leader. So this pig-eye lump of a man was the leader of the revolution. Tim felt a surge of disappointment for Lopez was anything but what he had pictured him. Tim had visualized a tall, clean cut man with a forceful personality and he felt cheated at what he saw.

As the general approached, Tim's captor drew himself to attention and saluted. Tim thought it might make a good impression if he did likewise. His hunch was right for he saw a flash of pleasure in the eyes of Lopez.

The general wasted few words.

"Who is this man?" he demanded of the other flyer. The pilot of the rebel plane told how he had sighted Tim and brought him to Cedros. He added that Tim had told him he hoped to join the rebel air force.

Lopez turned on Tim.

"So," he said, "you wish to join us."

Tim nodded.

"Who are you and where do you come from?" The words cracked through the air like a whiplash and Tim was startled by the forcefulness of the question but he had planned carefully for just such a moment.

"I'm Tim Murphy of Blanton," he replied, "and out for anything that promises good pay." Tim had decided to use his own name but not that of his home town.

Lopez was appraising him through half-closed eyes and Tim felt them boring into him, searching for something false in his appearance. Whatever the rebel chief's shortcomings might be, he was a man of decision.

"You can join us," he said, "at $200 a week, but one bad move and—." Lopez did not complete the sentence for a plane careened through the gap in the mountains and settled down swiftly on the field.

Tim, who was busy surveying his new surroundings, paid little attention to the newcomer until the pilot climbed out of his cockpit and took off his helmet.

Then he found himself staring into the eyes of Daredevil Dugan!

Before Tim had time to speak or motion Dugan to silence, the daredevil was striding toward him, hand outstretched.

"How's the flying reporter of the Atkinson News?" he cried.

Tim looked about him quickly. There wasn't a chance in the world for an escape. He'd have to face the music and he wondered if Dugan's words had been intended to get him into trouble.

"So!" the words hissed from Lopez' lips, "you're a flying reporter."

There was no use in denying and Tim felt that he might have a better chance if he told the truth. Without hesitation, he told who he was and why he had invaded the stronghold of the rebel chief.

"Well, well, well," drawled Lopez, "now isn't that nice of you to come down and see me. I'll be only too glad to pose for you. Suppose you get your camera out and take some pictures."

Tim wondered what the rebel's game was but he obeyed the orders and snapped Lopez in half a dozen different poses. The rebel leader's vanity irritated him and he would like to have punched his stubby little nose but that would only have spelled more trouble. When Lopez was satisfied that enough pictures had been taken, he turned accusing eyes on Dugan.

"And now Mr. Dugan," he said in a half whisper, "I thank you for telling me who this man is. He's not going back to the border and neither are you."

"What do you mean?" cried the daredevil "That you're not going back to the border. That's plain isn't it. Both of you know too much now. Besides, I never fully trusted you Dugan and this is a good excuse to put you out of the way."

"You can't get away with that," cried Dugan.

"Oh, I can't? Well, who's to stop me?" There seemed to be no immediate answer to that question and Tim and Dugan proceeded down the road in the direction of the village, two dirty little soldiers with drawn bayonets at their heels.

When they reached the plaza at Cedros, General Lopez ordered them thrown into the village jail, a filthy one-room structure with high, barred windows.

"You might have given me a break, Dugan," said Tim when the door had clanged shut on them. "There wasn't any special reason for your shouting my name all over the countryside, was there?"

"I'm mighty sorry about that, Tim," replied the daredevil and there was a convincing ring of sincerity to his words, "I was surprised to see you and didn't realize what I was saying."

"Do you think Lopez will keep us here long?"

"Think? I don't have to think. After what he said back there at the field, it may be curtains for us."

"He wouldn't dare put us out of the way for good," protested Tim.

"Yes, he would," replied the daredevil. "Lopez is in a desperate situation. If you took those pictures back to the border he would be instantly recognized when he tried to make his getaway. He'll go to any end to keep his pictures from being broadcast all over the U. S. A., and especially along the border."

"That's just what Captain Talbot of the border patrol at Nogales told me," said Tim. "He advised me not to make the trip down here and it commences to look like he was right."

"Talbot's got some fine flyers," said Dugan dryly. "One of them chased me for fifteen minutes when I crossed the border and shot my wings so full of holes I thought I was flying in a sieve."

Their conversation was interrupted when the door swung open and an officer ordered them to follow him. They were escorted across the plaza to the only hotel in the village, a straggling adobe structure where the rebel chieftain made his headquarters.

General Lopez wasted no words when they faced him.

"My council of war," he began as he pointed to a half dozen grinning officers at his side, "has decided that you are dangerous to our cause. This man," and he pointed at Tim, "has made a deliberate attempt to jeopardize my own life, while you," and he snapped the words at Dugan, "know too much for your own good."

The revolutionary leader paused for a moment to give weight to his next words.

"Therefore," he said slowly, enjoying every moment of the little drama in which he was the chief character, "the council has decreed that you shall die at sunrise tomorrow."

CHAPTER FOURTEEN

Tim, raging at the injustice of the whole thing, leaped, forward, his fists clenched, but Dugan caught his arms and whispered in his ear.

"Easy, Tim, easy. You'll only get a knife in your ribs."

Tim could see the truth in Dugan's words and allowed himself to be led back to the stinking little building which was dignified by the word "prison."

"Isn't there any way we can get word to the American authorities?" asked Tim.

"I'm afraid not," replied the daredevil. "Once a fellow comes below the border he's pretty much on his own and it's up to us to get out of here before daylight tomorrow. It won't be long before dark and then we'll see what can be done."

Tim, restless and angered by the events which had just taken place, paced about the room, testing the bars at the windows and kicking the dobe walls in an attempt to find some weakness. The idea of facing a firing squad in the morning did not strike him as especially alarming for he had confidence that in some way he and the daredevil would be able to make their escape.

The shadows of evening were already filling the plaza when Dugan went to a window and raised a shout for food. A guard ordered him to be silent, but he only increased his clamor until his cries attracted the attention of General Lopez, who was taking his evening stroll on the far side of the square.

"Provide them with food," ordered the rebel leader, "and see to it that it is a good meal for it will be their last."

The guard muttered under his breath but hastened away to carry out the command.

On one of his restless rounds of the room Tim's foot struck something half imbedded in the floor. He managed to pull the object free and found himself the possessor of a piece of iron pipe about eighteen inches long.

"Look here, Dugan," he exclaimed, "we ought to be able to dispose of Mr. Guard with this when he comes with our food."

"Give it to me," said the daredevil, "I want just one whack at that fellow's head."

"Not on your life," replied Tim. "I found the pipe and I'm perfectly capable of using it. You'll have your hands full if another guard happens along with this chap."

The guard could be heard returning and Tim took his place behind the door. His heart beat a trifle faster and he took a fresh grip on the pipe. He heard Dugan move closer.

"There's two of them," whispered the daredevil. "Let them both get inside and then use that pipe."

Tim heard one of the guards fumbling with the heavy lock, then the rattle of the chain, and finally the squeak of the rusty hinges as the door was swung open. The rays from a smoky kerosene lantern made a half-hearted attempt to pierce the gloom of their prison and the guard carrying the basket of food stepped into the room, followed by the man with the lantern. Before the rebels had a chance to get their eyes accustomed to the gloom, Tim leaped from his hiding place, his arm flashing in a quick blow that felled the man with the lantern before he could utter a cry of warning. Dugan caught the lantern as it dropped from the fingers of the unconscious soldier and Tim lunged ahead, bent on completing his task.

The man with the basket of food half turned. He saw Tim's upraised arm but was powerless to evade the blow. His cry of alarm was cut short and he fell limp into Tim's arms.

The whole thing had taken less than five seconds for Tim's two blows had been fast and true.

"Did you crack their heads?" asked Dugan.

"No," snapped Tim. "They'll be all right in a few minutes. We'd better get out of here and head for our planes. When they come to or are missed, this hotbed of rebels will be at our heels."

"Grab a blanket and sombrero from one of those chaps," said Dugan. "It will help us in getting out of the village."

Tim threw a blanket over his shoulders and pulled one of the high-crowned hats far down over his head.

"All right, let's go. You lead the way, Dugan."

The daredevil stepped outside their jail, pulled the door shut, rattled the chain, and then blew out the lantern. "Just in case anyone might be looking," he whispered to Tim. They melted into the shadows, and hurried in the direction of the field which served as headquarters for the rebel air force.

They reached the field unmolested and discarded their blankets.

"Better take my plane," suggested Tim. "It's fast and there's plenty of gas to get us to the border."

"Suits me," said Dugan. "The quicker we get away from here the better."

Tim climbed into the cockpit and his legs struck something boxlike as he swung into his seat. His groping hands discovered his camera. He could hardly repress a shout for there was his machine loaded with the pictures for which Lopez had so arrogantly posed in the afternoon. Tim recalled having seen an officer drop the camera back into the cockpit of his plane. What rare luck.

Tim placed the heavy camera under his seat and turned on the light over his instrument board for a moment to be sure that the delicate gauges and his compass had not been tampered. Satisfied that everything was all right, he called down to Dugan to hop aboard.

"In just a minute, Tim," said the daredevil. "There are a couple of planes here and Lopez may send them out after us when he realizes we have escaped. It will be moonlight in a few minutes and we don't want to take any chances of being overhauled and shot down."

He slipped away and a moment later Tim heard the sound of a heavy blow and splintering of wood. In a few seconds the sound was repeated and then Dugan appeared beside the Good News chuckling.

"Neither one of those ships will get into the air tonight," he said. "I found a heavy club and smashed their props."

Dugan took his place in the forward cockpit and Tim bent down to turn on the starter. Just then he heard shouts and cries of alarm from the village and lanterns flashed in the trees that separated the field from Lopez' headquarters.

"Get going, Tim, get going," urged Dugan. "They've found out we've escaped. You've got about a thousand feet of level ground ahead. Then you'll have to lift her fast to clear the trees."

Tim turned on the starter and it whirred for what seemed an age while the dancing lanterns came closer.

Finally the motor caught and burst into a roar that reverberated down the valley. There was no time to warm up the engine and Tim opened his throttle and sped his plane down the field.

Faster and faster they raced while behind them the night was punctuated with crimson stabs of rifle fire as the rebels sent volley after volley crashing in pursuit of the fleeing plane.

The motor never faltered and when the trees loomed ahead Tim had plenty of flying speed. He zoomed the Good News into the night sky and turned on his instrument light to get his bearings.

Ahead of him he could discern the gap in the mountains and he roared through it with his exhaust belching streams of flame.

Tim set his course for Nogales, north by west and settled down for three hours of flying. By the time the moon came up, Sonora was far to their rear and a few minutes after midnight they circled the field at Nogales. The sound of their motor awakened the field crew and landing lights were turned on.

When Tim brought the Good News to a stop, he was greeted by Captain Talbot, who had thrown a coat on over his pajamas.

"Back already?" he asked.

"Back and with half a dozen pictures posed by General Lopez," grinned Tim.

"What!" exclaimed the army man, who could hardly believe what he had heard.

Tim pulled his camera out from under his seat. "Right here," he said, "are half a dozen of first class pictures of Lopez. Let's go into the office," he added, "and I'll tell you all about it."

Captain Talbot was almost incredulous when he heard Tim's story but the plates were absolute proof of his tale.

"I'll leave one of the plates with you for your border patrol bulletin," said Tim, "but the pictures must be kept in strict confidence. Now if I can get some gas I think we'll hop along toward Atkinson. If we can get away from here at 1 o'clock we ought to make it there by noon tomorrow, figuring on one more stop for gas and oil."

"Dugan going to help you pilot on the way home?" asked Captain Talbot.

"Yes," said Tim, "and I'll need the help."

"I expect you will. I ought to hold Dugan here under arrest but I guess he's learned his lesson and won't go hunting for any more revolutions. How about it Dugan?"

"You're right, Captain Talbot. No more revolutions for mine."

"If I can borrow a control stick for the front cockpit it will help out a lot," suggested Tim.

"I'll have the boys put one in right away," said the genial captain.

While the Good News was being made ready for its thousand mile flight to Atkinson, Tim wired Carson that he was on his way with the plates and would arrive about noon the next day.

At one a. m. Tim and Dugan sped away from the Nogales field and their friends of the border patrol. Dawn found them well on their way toward Atkinson and at 11:30 o'clock Tim sighted his home field.

When they taxied up to the apron, Tim found Carson waiting for him.

The managing editor had ordered a dark room for developing the plates rigged up at the field and in less than half an hour, a complete set of pictures were on their way to the News office while another set, still damp, were placed on board a special plane to be rushed to Chicago where they were to be placed on the telephoto wires.

Tim had written the story of his adventure while Dugan had handled the controls and the story of his flight and the pictures of the rebel leader were on the front page of the first afternoon edition of the News—a clean beat over every other paper in the country.

Tim was preparing to leave the field when Dugan stopped him,

"Can you spare a minute?" he asked, his voice low and tense. He was evidently laboring under great emotion and Tim followed him toward the field and away from the others.

"I haven't forgotten how you saved me the day the good will tour ended here," hastened Dugan, "nor what you've done this time and I'll repay you now. You've heard of the Sky Hawk?"

Tim nodded, waiting for the other to go on.

"I know who he is," went on Dugan, his voice hoarse from emotion. "He's a former German ace, a great flyer, but obsessed with the idea that by plundering the air lines he can amass a great fortune and eventually attack America from the air. It's a crazy dream—a wild one—but he's sure raising hob while he's free."

"He certainly is," agreed Tim. "Who is it, Dugan?" He waited for the answer, hardly breathing.

The daredevil's lips started to move. Then he glanced toward the sky where a heavy humming drifted down.

A plane shot through the clouds, whipped around and headed in for the field. The crescendo of its motor was deafening; conversation was impossible. Dugan screamed something at Tim but the words were inaudible. Then he started running along the field in front of the hangers.

Tim yelled after him but his words were lost in the storm of noise as the plane skimmed over the field. The flying reporter screamed until he thought his lungs would burst. Dugan, running toward the Good News, was sprinting directly into the path of the incoming plane.

There was a blur of light, a form hurtling through the air.

The pilot of the plane leaped from his ship. There was something familiar in his build—in his stride. When they reached Dugan he was beyond help and Tim stared across the body of the daredevil into the hard eyes of Kurt Blandin.

CHAPTER FIFTEEN

Later in the day Kurt Blandin stalked into the News office and went directly to Tim's desk.

"Too bad about Dugan," he said, but there was no pity in his words. "I didn't see him until we struck. I'd thought of bringing the air circus back here, but I'm not so sure about it now. The accident will give us kind of a black eye."

"You don't seem to be very sorry about what happened to Dugan," snapped Tim, his eyes steely and his lips drawn in hard lines. "And Blandin, I don't think we want you around here. There are a lot of things you are going to have to explain. I've got a few suspicions about you that aren't very pleasant—Sky Hawk!"

The last words fairly ripped between Tim's lips. Tensed, the flying reporter watched their effect on Blandin. The head of the Ace air circus swayed like a slender reed in the wind, but there was no change in the mask-like expression of his face. Perhaps his eyes shifted slightly, but that was all. He laughed, a cold, nerve-chilling laugh that shocked Tim's finer sensibilities.

"You're crazy, Murphy," replied Blandin and before Tim could reply, turned and hurried from the room.

For half an hour Tim remained at his desk, mulling over the events of the last months. Only a few hours before he had been so near the solution—so near to learning the identity of the Sky Hawk. If Dugan could only talk, but Dugan's lips were stilled forever.

The daredevil's words about the German ace came back to him and he went into the library in the News building and sat down before a large file. Slowly he thumbed through the orderly stack of pictures with their descriptive stories attached. Back through the years he went as he rejected first one picture and then another.

Suddenly he stopped. The picture in his hand was familiar. A face was smiling up at him from the glossy print, a German fatigue cap was set at a jaunty angle, there was a slight scar over one eye—it was familiar and yet unfamiliar. It looked like Kurt Blandin, yet it was unlike Kurt Blandin. It might have been Kurt ten years before.

Hastily Tim read the short paragraph of descriptive matter attached. The picture in his hand was that of Max Reuter, one of the greatest of

German aces, who had been brought down behind the Allied lines just before the close of the war. Shell-shocked, Reuter had been held in a prison camp until the close of the war and then released.

The clipping told little more of importance, but to Tim it had provided a world of information. The whole puzzle fitted together. Dugan's story, even without him, was complete, and he hurried from the library and started toward the municipal airport.

Tim had a premonition of danger and when he reached the field was not surprised to see Hunter run toward him the minute he came through the gate.

"Tim, Tim," cried the field manager. "The Sky Hawk has struck! He's wrecked our eastbound express plane and looted its cargo!"

"Where?" asked Tim with a numbness of heart that seemed to weigh him down.

"East of Montour. The report just came in. It couldn't have happened more than an hour ago. Ralph's over on the line now warming up your ship. Will you help us out?"

Tim nodded, hastened into the office for a suit of coveralls and in five minutes was speeding west. Less than an hour later they were scudding to a landing on a field where the remains of the eastbound express were only a blackened heap.

It was a simple story. The country was sparsely settled. A forced landing by the plane, a pounce by the waiting Sky Hawk, a dead pilot, a flaming plane with empty express compartments. The marks of the Sky Hawk's plane were plainly visible in the snow, even his footprints could be discerned. But that was all There were no fingerprints, nothing more than the tracks in the snow. It looked like a hopeless quest when Ralph, poking around in the wreckage of the plane, picked up a bit of metal. It was a small piece of copper, corroded, strangely so.

Without explaining his action to Tim, he pocketed it and they prepared for the return flight to Atkinson.

"Find out anything?" demanded Hunter who was waiting for them when they landed.

"Not much," said Ralph, "but I'm going to ride the westbound plane tomorrow morning. Maybe we'll know more then."

"What's this theory about the Sky Hawk you're working on?" asked Tim when they were alone.

"It's hardly a theory," admitted Ralph. "A hunch maybe, but not a theory. Look at this."

He pulled the chunk of corroded copper from his pocket.

"It's one of the cabin fittings," said Tim recognizing the piece from the wrecked plane, "but what of it."

"Nothing much," replied Ralph, "except it holds the secret of the Sky Hawk's power."

"What! You're crazy."

"No, I'm not crazy. It's as plain as day. You wait and see."

"I'll wait, all right," agreed Tim. "Either you're awful bright or I'm awfully dumb. But this is your show. You must have a good idea of how the Sky Hawk is bringing down these planes. Here's luck."

The next morning found them at the field, ready for the departure of the westbound express. Hunter, worried and anxious, was on hand. Every plane which the Sky Hawk destroyed meant a loss of $25,000 and he could see a year's profits gone in a week unless someone solved the secret of the Sky Hawk's power.

Tim was warming up the Good News but turned for a final word from Ralph.

"Fly high and keep well behind us," instructed his chum. "If anything goes wrong with our ship, cut your motor, listen for the hum of another plane, but don't try to follow it. Beat it for the ground and pull what's left of us clear of the machine."

"And don't," he added as an after thought, "dive through any queer looking clouds which may be near our plane if we're struck down."

With that Ralph hurried into the cockpit of the waiting express ship where he crowded in beside the pilot. In another minute both planes were winging their way into the west, the motors barking in the cold winter air.

The trip was uneventful and four hours later the planes roared down on the snow covered field at Lytton, the western terminal of the transcontinental's southwestern division.

"Too clear. We need clouds to catch the Sky Hawk," was the only explanation Ralph would make when Tim asked him about the trip.

The next day Ralph looked at the winter sky, studded with scurrying wind-swept clouds.

"We'll go with the express," he informed Hunter over the phone. "The Sky Hawk will strike today and we want to be on the job."

Ralph lapsed into a grim silence as Tim and the pilot of the express ship prepared their planes for the takeoff on the eastbound trip. Within a few hours, perhaps minutes, the Sky Hawk would strike again. Just where and how he could only guess. He was pitting his nerve and brains against the craft of a master crook. The decision was in the balance.

Ralph conferred with Tim for a moment before he crowded into the cockpit of the express plane. Then the two ships whirled over the snow and into the air.

An hour, two hours elapsed and the planes were speeding over the desolate Rock river country.

Tim, above and behind the mail, suddenly saw the express plane wobble unsteadily and then drop away in a sickening dive. Remembering the instructions Ralph had given him, he cut the motor of his own craft, and glided noiselessly through the broken clouds. He thought he heard the faint hum of a motor—a higher pitched note than that of the express plane's engine. It was gone in a second and he turned his attention to the express plane, fluttering helplessly toward the ground.

With motor on full, he crashed downward through the clouds in a screaming power dive. Every strut on the Good News shrilled its protest but he held the nose down. He must reach the ground with the express; must be able to help Ralph and the express pilot if they needed his assistance.

The express was limping toward a small clearing and Tim, now under it, leveled off and made a fast landing. A ground loop slowed his speed and he was running toward the express plane when it banged down into the snow, its landing gear crumpling as the pilot made clumsy attempt to land. The plane flipped over on its nose and a figure was thrown clear of the wreckage.

Tim reached the limp form on the snow. It was Ralph! But there was no time to ascertain how badly his chum was injured. There was a sizzling flash, a roar, and the motor of the express was enveloped in a mass of flame. Tim plunged on and under the overturned fuselage. There, still strapped in his seat, he found the unconscious pilot. With anxious hands he unfastened the safety belt and dragged the man away from the flaming craft.

When he returned to Ralph, he found his chum gasping for air but otherwise unhurt. Together they worked to bring the express pilot back to consciousness.

"What happened?" demanded Tim.

"The Sky Hawk almost got us," said Ralph, his voice husky and unnatural. "Another ten seconds and our goose would have been cooked. Here, let's get this chap in the Good News. We've got to get him to a doctor quick. I'll tell you all about it on the way to Atkinson."

When they were safely on their way to the home field, Ralph explained what had happened.

"He gassed us," he said simply. "That's the secret of his power to send planes and pilots to their destruction. He only strikes on cloudy days when he can hide in the clouds. Just before his intended victim comes along, he releases the gas in the clouds. The unsuspecting pilot runs right into the gas and puff! That's all there is to it. Simple, isn't it?"

Tim was speechless with the horror of the Sky Hawk's method.

"Simple, yes," he managed to say, "but terrible."

"I'll admit that," grinned Ralph, and after tomorrow, if the weather's cloudy, there won't be any more Sky Hawk.

"What do you mean?"

"That we'll get the Sky Hawk. Now that we know his methods, we have the upper hand. This terror of the skies is about at the end of his string."

When they landed at Atkinson a doctor quickly brought the express flyer back to consciousness although he was rushed to a hospital for treatment to check the ravages of the gas which he had breathed. Ralph had been lucky and the slight whiff he had gotten had knocked him out only temporarily with no lasting danger.

They reported to Hunter, studied the weather forecasts for the next day, and completed their simple preparations for the capture of the Sky Hawk.

The morning edition of the News carried a carefully worded story how a special plane was to leave Atkinson that morning on a dash across the plains with a heavy shipment of specie needed by a bank at the western terminal of the division. The $1,000,000 plane, the paper called it.

When Tim and Ralph wheeled the Good News from the hangar that morning, a truck was coming through the main gate with uniformed policemen on the running boards. It was the work only of a minute to transfer the two dummy specie chests, heavy iron-bound boxes, from the truck to the cabin of the Good News. They were leaving nothing to chance for the Sky Hawk might have accomplices on the field.

After a word with Hunter, Tim gunned the motor of the Good News and they raced across the field and into the air in quest of the Sky Hawk. Both boys were concentrating on the task ahead.

When they neared the Rock River country Ralph nudged his companion.

"Better put on the gas masks," he warned. "The clouds are heavy ahead of us; just the place for the Sky Hawk."

They donned the gas protectors, ready for the Sky Hawk to strike. Ahead of them loomed a cloud, grayish-green in color.

Ralph signed for Tim to cut the motor. They soared silently. To their right and ahead of them they could hear the sound of another plane. Tim turned on his motor and ruddered hard to the right. All around them were the grayish-green clouds of gas. The Sky Hawk had laid a careful trap for the specie plane.

Suddenly they broke through the clouds. Just ahead of them a sleek, black monoplane was loafing in the sky. Its pilot, startled at the sudden appearance of the Good News, was caught unawares, and they were almost on him before he could rev up his motor.

As they roared down on the monoplane, they caught a glimpse of the pilot, his face covered with a hideous mask to protect him from the gas clouds which he had scattered through the sky.

It was the Sky Hawk, the terror of the airways!

With quickening pulse, Tim set himself to the task of riding the Sky Hawk to earth. He knew his plane was faster than that of the aerial bandit, but could he match his skill with the enemy and force him to earth?

There was a puff of smoke under the fuselage of the Sky Hawk's plane and another of the gray-green clouds took form. But Tim and Ralph were protected from the gas and they drove through the cloud in a burst of speed.

The Sky Hawk looked around, plainly alarmed. He had evidently believed their, first appearance pure luck but their escape this time was no such thing and the sky bandit realized that he was cornered. He could fight or run and either way the odds were against him for the Good News was too speedy for his craft. The tables were turned on the Sky Hawk. For the first time he found the odds against him and he chose to run.

It was a game to Tim's liking and he roared down on the tail of the black monoplane. Both Tim and Ralph were armed but they hesitated to use their guns except as a last resort.

On and on they roared, first zig-zagging to the right, then to the left, up, then down, always on the tail of the sky Hawk, driving him ever nearer the ground.

Desperate, the masked bandit in the black plane turned on them and bullet after bullet ripped through the air as he blazed away at Tim and Ralph with a sub-machine gun. It was dangerous work now, but Tim handled the Good News in masterful fashion relentlessly teasing the Sky Hawk into shooting at them when they had him at a disadvantage.

Finally the sky bandit threw away his gun, his ammunition exhausted. Tim saw the gesture and steeled himself for the end. Whatever its outcome it would come quickly.

The Sky Hawk threw his plane into a crazy, twisting climb that threatened to pull the motor out of the ship. Tim outguessed him and climbed two feet to the bandit's one. Two, three, four, five thousand feet they clawed their way into the sky, the Sky Hawk trying frantically to escape his pursuers for in the grimfaced flying reporters he could read his finish unless escape came soon.

Ralph had put together the tangled webs which put them on the Sky Hawk's trail. Now it was up to Tim to bring about the end of the career of the gangster of the airways.

"Hang on," yelled Tim as he pushed the throttle to the end of its arc. The song of the motor deepened and the Good News quivered as it felt the full power of the 500 horse power engine.

The Good News dropped down on the Sky Hawk's ship like an avenging eagle. It swooped low, ready for the kill.

Closer and closer came the motor-maddened planes, each pilot intent on the destruction of the other. Then, too late to escape, the Sky Hawk guessed Tim's plan but before he could move or throw his plane into a spin, there was the crash of wood and the scream of wires.

Half of the upper wing of the monoplane crumpled as Tim raked his landing gear through it. The propeller shivered into a thousand pieces and the motor raced madly.

Tim and Ralph, peering from their plane, saw the black craft pause in mid-air for a moment. In that fleeting second they saw the Sky Hawk half rise in his cockpit and rip the gas mask from his face.

It was Kurt Blandin and in the anger-marked face Tim recognized the likeness to Max Reuter, the German ace. The mystery was solved, the puzzle fitted and Blandin punctuated its completion with a final show of bravado as he raised clenched fists toward them.

Then the black plane fell away in a tight spin. Blandin made no effort to escape and a thousand feet above the ground the wings collapsed and the Sky Hawk crashed to his death.

Tim swung the Good News in a great circle, then headed for Atkinson. The Sky Hawk was gone; the airways were clear once more.

Milton Keynes UK
Ingram Content Group UK Ltd.
UKHW040700150224
437844UK00007B/678